Highlander's Holly and Ivy

by

Margaret Izard

Stones of Iona

Highlander's Holly and Ivy

COPYRIGHT © 2025 by Margaret Izard

Cover Art by *Lisa Dawn MacDonald*

The Wild Rose Press, Inc.
PO Box 708
Adams Basin, NY 14410-0708
Visit us at www.thewildrosepress.com

Publishing History
First Edition, 2025
Trade Paperback ISBN 978-1-5092-6152-9
Digital ISBN 978-1-5092-6153-6

Stones of Iona
Published in the United States of America

Dedication

To my husband, your unwavering support, endless patience, and belief in me have been the foundation of this dream. Thank you for being my rock and my biggest fan.

To my children, your boundless imagination and love remind me daily that anything is possible. You are my greatest inspiration.

This book is for all of you—my heart, home, and everything.

Chapter 1

Sweat trickled down Alex's spine as a crushing sense of obligation seized him. He rose to answer Scotland's call—the land he owed a debt so immense his duty weighed on every step he took. No matter the task, he knew he could never truly repay what was due. For years, he and his da had clashed over that very burden, yet Alex could never see himself as worthy enough to right the terrible wrong.

Memories hit Alex like a punch in the gut. He pictured himself sneaking into his parents' bedroom, taking the MacDougall heart necklace—the one each Lady MacDougall wore for generations. The memory flipped like a page.

He stood on the hillside, Heather MacEwen before him. "I love ye, Alex."

He smiled. "And I ye." They wrapped their hands in a cloth he'd brought for the handfasting ceremony. Alex's heart beat hard, but his love for her blossomed.

Alex whispered. "I pledge myself to ye, Heather."

She replied, "I take ye, my beloved, into my heart. I pledge myself to ye, Alex."

He leaned his forehead on hers. "I take ye, my beloved, into my heart." They kissed and unwrapped their hands.

Alex placed the necklace over Heather's head. "The Stone of Love, Heather. The Fae stone I told ye the fable of. Ye are my true love, and it will now glow." But the stone didn't glow that day, not for Heather and not for him. He'd flipped open the pendant, and the dark red stone lay still.

The air churned around them, and a sinister laugh filled the area. "Silly boy, ye must have yer true love to make that stone work." A man in all black flew at them, his hand thrust out, and a powerful push of air knocked Heather to the ground. Alex bent over her as she tried to breathe. Her eyes connected with his, and blood flowed from her mouth. Her face now frozen in death.

Alex picked up the Stone of Love and held the gem before him. "I banish ye to hell, evil Fae!"

The man landed before him. "Foolish boy. Ye cannot power that stone without love."

The evil man flicked his wrist, and the stone flew to him. "Tell Dagda, Balor sends his regards. I have one Stone of Iona. Soon, the others will be mine and the realms mine to rule."

Alex crumpled over Heather's body.

The memory faded as he stood rigid. His failure to protect the sacred Iona Stone still tore at his heart, an ache so deep the pain had extinguished any hope of him finding love. He had failed—not just the Fae, but his family, his people. He wasn't strong enough to uphold the vow his bloodline to the Fae had sworn to mankind— to shield the Fae Stones from evil's clutches.

Scotland paid the price for his weakness. The land he loved, broken and suffering, bore the scars of his mistakes. Guilt gnawed at his soul, but his agony also fueled his resolve. Redemption became his only purpose, his singular obsession. He had begged for this new duty—a chance to heal the wounds he'd caused and bridge the bitter divide between the ruling English and the defiant Scots. His obligation was a challenging path that demanded he sacrifice much, but for him, this was the only way to reclaim his honor.

The gavel's echo jolted Alex to attention in Glasgow's courtroom—a place as familiar to him as his own home.

The Scottish woman waved at the British Lord beside her. "Aye, Mi'Lord, I knocked on his door. Asked right like, and the dodger wouldn't let me go piss!" Mabina McGee could be a pain sometimes, but she was the best baker in Glasgow, Scotland. Hell, even the English favored her shortbread over anyone else's, and her mince pies nearly melted in your mouth. Rumor had it the popular High Tea Room on Argyle Street was *the place* for luncheon, but you'd never catch an Englishman admitting as much.

The people in the courtroom erupted in guffaws. Lord James Charles Peter Stourton, Baron Mowbray straightened his dress coat. "Certainly, I shall not have to be forced to allow every beggar in Scotland the use of my loo. She forced herself into my home, and well…you know." The Lord waved his hands to his side as more laughter came from the room.

Lord James Erskine, Lord Advocate of Scotland, pinched his nose and turned to him. "Alex, by all that is holy, please explain to me what she means?"

Alex MacDougall, Lord Justice Clerk to Scotland, covered his mouth to stop laughing. While his job was to bridge the gap between the newly ordained English and Scottish law, the right to ask to use one's *facilities* falling under the old law of *hospitality* might stretch his duties a bit.

He now crossed the courtroom, to stand between Mabina and Lord Mowbray. Alex spoke in the proper English cadence he often used in the courtroom. "It's an older custom that falls under hospitality. Allowing the use of one's facilities is one showing hospitality." He glanced at Mabina, who winked at him. "I am sure Mrs. McGee meant no harm."

She nodded at him.

He waved to the Englishman. "And I am sure Lord Mowbray is a true gentleman and merely wasn't educated in our…unusual custom."

Lord Mowbray huffed, "My Lord, certainly you will punish such an act. She practically broke into my home."

Mabina cried out, "I did not. Ye held yer door open, and when I asked to use yer pisser, ye closed the door on me." She held her arm up. "Nearly broke my arm, he did. How am I to make me pies now?"

The complainant yelled, "She's a criminal! They are all criminals! How is a proper gentleman to conduct business in this land of outlaws and savages!" Everyone in the room yelled back and forth. The English pitted against the Scots. Would there ever be a day this would end? That they all could get along and work side by side peaceably?

The Justice yelled, "Silence!" All in the courtroom fell quiet. He rubbed his forehead. "Alex, is this truly a law?"

All the room turned to him. "Written, well indirectly, yes, sir. It's a practice that's more of a courtesy."

Lord Mowbray waved his hand. "I came here to trade and sell tobacco, not embed myself in their swine culture."

Pig culture. Well, that was a new one. As Alex raised his face to Lord Erskine, he feared what James might do with Mowbray. More and more Englishmen came for business as the Scots recently gained new trade routes with the Americas that looked to turn into very profitable ventures for all.

Lord Erskine took a deep breath. "Lord Mowbray, James, correct me if I am wrong, but this *pig culture* and *savage race* you cannot abide, aren't they providing for your very lucrative venture? Don't they gather their tobacco leaves for you from the American ships and then sell them for a considerable profit you pocket?"

The Englishman in question pulled on his coat sleeves. "Yes, your lord."

Justice Erskine smiled. "Then might I suggest you practice a little more *hospitality* to these swine, savage people, or you might find yourself back in England, penniless!"

Erskine swung his gavel and called out, "Not guilty."

Mabina grabbed Alex's arm. "Thank ye, Alex. He was a right skinny bassa, wasn't he?" Alex patted her hand and nodded, knowing Lord Mowbray stood within hearing distance.

The baker tapped his shoulder. "Yer a right good one ye are, regardless of what they say about yer clan. Running from Culloden over burnt feet. Bah." She turned away, then twisted back, whispering, "I will see ye tonight at the Gaels Meeting?" She bent closer and gave the Gaels signal, a finger sticking out of the forehead for the Scottish unicorn. "Next to the slaughterhouse like we do every week?"

Smarting over the comment of the well-known

reason his clan didn't fight at Culloden, he still smiled. The Gaels were something he was very proud of. Their secret meetings where Scots gathered, wore the outlawed plaids, and spoke in Gaelic about the old days and how to move forward in the new English-ruled world of Scotland were the highlight of every week. They met at a railway bridge near the slaughterhouse. While the area stunk to high heaven, this was a place the British officers wouldn't dare go near.

He patted her hand as he removed it from his arm, uttering in his native cadence. "Aye, now go along before the Sassenach declares ye broke another law."

She turned. "Stop by the shop later for a pie, laddie. We all luv the work ye do keeping Scots laws alive."

Alex bent to her, whispering, "I'll try, but I've got a full case load today. It may be hours."

Mabina patted his arm. "Don't work too hard." Alex nodded and moved back to his seat for the next case.

The bailiff stood and called, "Lord Comfrey brings charges against the highland beggar for eating his trash." Alex pinched his nose, wondering when the English would finally call them *people*. Another five cases, all English accusing Scots of something absurd, and Alex finished for the day.

Lord Erskine stepped down from his high seat. "Alex, my boy, another day saving the Scots." He patted his shoulder. "I do appreciate all you do. It is a huge help." He sighed. "One day, maybe we'll have real legal cases."

Alex smiled. He truly liked the Englishman sent to hold law over Glasgow in the new modern English-ruled Scotland. The man listened and ruled with an honest and sympathetic heart. Alex suspected he truly wanted peace and a unified city rather than what most Englishmen wanted—complete control and annihilation of all that was Scottish.

The lord walked away and called over his shoulder, "Come by the manor and dine with us tonight."

Alex grinned. "Thank you, sir. Another time—I have plans this evening."

Lord Erskine winked as he turned to the door. "Well, then, I wish the fine lady well."

He shrugged. "Not a lady, but thank you all the same."

In the emptying courtroom, he reflected on his path in life. After years of law school in Glasgow, Alex dreamed of becoming a solicitor. With the threat of the Jacobite rising behind them, he finally had his chance at the best duty he could hope for, Lord Justice Clerk to Scotland and bridging the gap between the English and Scottish law. He strode through the doors into the entryway, still filled with people milling about after the day's cases. Erskine mentioning a lady burned his heart, a reminder of his failure. He shook the memory off as he pushed out the outer doors, swung his cloak over his shoulders to avoid the cold, and trod to where John MacArthur stood with Oberon, his black war horse.

John nodded as he approached. "Another fun day at the gallows of Scotland?"

Alex put his gloves on and took the reins. "Argued over piss today." He mounted and came up beside his longtime friend. "If the English Lord had had his way, Mabina would be beheaded for pissing in his loo."

John's eyebrows rose high. "Not Mabina McGee? Where would Glasgow eat?"

Alex's stomach growled. "Aye. The lord even called

us a swine culture."

His friend chuckled. "Mabina makes great pork pies as well as mince pies."

As Alex kneed Oberon into a trot he said, "Promised me dinner, Mabina did."

John caught up with him. "Don't have time, Alex. Ye're due to lead the meetin' tonight. Yer plaid is in yer saddle bag. And yer flask is in yer sporran." They rode out of the square onto the newly built Queens Street and headed to the slaughterhouse or the bridge near there where the Gaels meeting took place. Behind him, the Cow Lane ran north between the Meadow flat lands, to the west, and the Ramshorn croft cleared for further stone homes and business development. While parts of Scotland didn't do well after the Jacobite rebellion's fall, Glasgow thrived into a modern bustling port. Since seventeen fifty, three years of wealth from the tobacco, sugar, and cotton trade brought rapid expansion westward. New streets were laid out just this year, including Argyle Street and Virginia Street. Miller Street was in the future plans.

They turned and headed east on High Street and rode quickly past all the newer businesses and homes. Candles lit many of the windows decorated early for Yule. Home doors sported evergreen wreaths with candles decorating the circles. The yule time, or as the protestants called it Christmas, was his favorite. His mother decorated like no one he'd seen. Mistletoe tucked into greenery covered every surface. Memories of happier times with his family warmed his heart.

Soon, they came upon the bridge under the rail tracks, and Sheriff Drake stood at his normal post outside the bridge at the small brazier. "Ho, Alex! Mabina's already back singing your praise. She tells everyone you got her free today. She gave out pies." He rubbed his stomach. "I do love her pies."

Alex and John rode forward and dismounted near the firepit.

A street boy Alex recognized rushed forward. "Hold them for ye, laird?"

He ruffled the lad's hair. "Aye, Jimmy. How's yer ma?" John dismounted as they unpacked their plaids and sporrans, wrapping them quickly over their trews.

Jimmy grinned as he took the reins and led the horses to the water trough. "Better, and me Da's inside waiting for ye as are the others. I got a pie from Mabina!"

Officer Drake stopped Alex with a hand on his arm. "Lt. Tytler is on the hunt again. He tried to take my post, claiming you are all Jacobites raising a rebellion again. Be careful. I know you are only out here keeping the Scots going, forging a path for them to follow so the English and Scots live in peace."

Alex patted his hand. "Thanks for the warning. I'll keep an eye out."

Turning he nodded to Jimmy. "Keep them warm, and I'll have an extra shilling for ye." He buckled his sporran into place and reached inside, grabbing his flask.

He turned to John. "'Tis time." John smiled and nodded.

As he strode under the bridge into the large crowd, he raised his flask, and shouted, "Sláinte!"

The crowd replied, "Sláinte!"

Alex gulped from his flask, and his da's whisky rolled down smoothly. "To the new Scotland! New trade, new business, and a new city!"

The crowd replied, "Aye!"

He nodded. "Take yer ease, Gaels, visit and enjoy yer time as Scots." Many around him began conversing in Gaelic. Most men wore their plaids as the women huddled under their arisaids. He took comfort in knowing that he led the group in their secret meeting to hold to their culture, the Highland ways.

Mabina approached with a wrapped bundle. "Ye didn't make it past my shop. So, I made ye a packet. Eat up, lad. Ye earned it well this day." The fresh scent of mince pie wafted to his nose, making his stomach rumble. He hadn't had anything since the nooning. A busy day it had been. He moved off to the other side of the bridge, farther away from the crowd, to find some quiet time alone.

As Alex leaned against the railing, noises from the pub beside him rose and then fell. He pulled out a pie and bit into it, the spiced meat curbing his hunger as he ate. People bustled by, coming and going to what and where he didn't care.

A petite young woman in pale blue marched by. Her maid followed with packages. The young beauty's gaze caught his, and she slowed. Their eyes connected across the busy street. Her heart-shaped face framed by her light blue cloak appeared angelic, the setting sun casting a glow on skin pink from the chill.

Time slowed as he stood transfixed by her stare. An auburn curl escaped and blew across her face. His desire to brush the wayward strand away nearly had him crossing the street to her. She blinked, and the maid ran into her, jostling the packages.

A beauty for sure, but for him, no. He turned from the woman, giving her his back like he did all women these days. The burn of failure crept into his heart. The betrayal and pain resurfaced from the deep place he'd buried them. In his world, romance and love were a complication best left alone. When he turned, John's sympathetic expression met his.

His eyes roamed over Alex's shoulder. "A beauty, and she still stares."

"Let her."

John grabbed his arm. "Ye will have to deal with this sooner or later, Alex. Ye will be the laird one day. Leadership, a wife, offspring, and all that duty entails will fall to ye."

He handed John the last pie. "Have one of Mabina's pies, John."

Someone from the crowd called out, "Alex, a toast!"

Alex raised his flask. "To whisky and Scotland!"

They all raised their drinks. "Aye!"

Hours later, Alex stumbled into his townhouse in New Town Glasgow. His home greeted him with the same familiar darkness each day.

As John came in behind him, the fire burned low in the parlor. "That was a quick ride in the dark. Didn't even bother to remove our plaids. I'm off to bed." His friend climbed the stairs. "George took care of the horses." He yawned as he rounded the first turn. "Tomorrow comes too soon." Then called down, "Bertha will be up with yer Scots breakfast before court."

Alex waited till the opening and closing of John's door resounded before he entered the room, thankful John hadn't noticed the visitor seated in his favorite chair before the fire. He ambled to the fireplace and stood beside the man. A familiar walking cane rested beside him.

His visitor held a snifter of whisky and took a sip.

"No warm greeting for yer father?"

Alex sighed. "Hello, Da."

He glanced at his father. He'd gained more gray hair, and his aged skin reflected in the fire's warm glow, making him look older and worn.

Roderick MacDougall, Laird of clan MacDougall, took a deep breath. "Ye tempt fate running around in yer plaid, son. Ye'd gain more favor in yer trews than yer tartan." He chuckled, "Although I hear Lord Lovat is beside himself with anger that his son, while at Glasgow University under a Campbell's tutelage, has taken to dressing and acting like a fop. Lovet claims he's all trussed up in silks, walking around like a woman." He nodded. "At least ye still know how to dress like a man."

Alex grinned. He hated the new dress for men— perfumes and silks. While he kept a more regular grooming routine than others, he still dressed manly. Thankfully, he had not had the courtesy of tutoring directly under a Campbell, but instead served as a house boy to a lesser teacher who was kinder in his treatment.

His da took another sip before setting the flask down and handing a chest to Alex. The heavy weight had him holding the small trunk with both hands.

A sober tone filled his da's voice. "Open it, son."

Alex pulled the lever aside, released the lid, and lifted it. Inside was a blue diamond-shaped stone resting atop a long, bright green, rectangular stone set in a large pin. Both gems winked in the firelight bringing back memories better left in the past. His love for Heather— her dying body in his arms—Balor's taunting remarks, all still stung these years later.

Alex blinked as the memory faded, leaving him rocked as he stood staring at the two other Stones of Iona, the Stone of Faith and the Stone of Hope.

His father took a deep breath. "Ye gaze upon the Brooch of Lorne, son. Yer time to serve and yer purpose is at hand."

Alex stared at the two stones as dread filled his heart. "No. I will not do this."

His father whacked his cane against the fireplace. "Ye touched the Stone of Love. Ye are the guardian now. Ye must take yer place and find the stone before none of Scotland is left. Balor punishes Scotland for our protection of the stones." He rose and limped across the room, his cane thumping every other step. "Ye must find the Stone of Love and restore it to the chapel."

Alex slammed the chest's lid. "At what sacrifice? Another life stolen for the stones. I am to find true love only to have her taken again?" He set the box on the mantel, rested his hand sensing the magic stones' powers, then yanked his palm away, denying the stones' existence.

His father thumped his cane onto the floor. "We all make sacrifices. Now Dagda, King of the Tuatha Dé Danann, has ordered us to seal the crypt and allow yer mother's chapel to fall into ruin so the evil Fae won't know where the stones are." He stood resting on his cane. "Yer mother's heart is near broken in grief. We fell in love in that chapel. Renewed our vows there." He sighed heavily. "We baptized ye there after we solved the riddle of the attempted stabbing of yer mother." His father stood taller, pointing a finger at him. "Even yer future family, Colin and Bree MacDougall from the twentieth century who risked their fate for me and yer mother— aided in yer future—fell in love there!"

Alex paced. "Time travel I have not seen. Future and

past folding over into one." He stopped slashing his hand to the side. "No! The Fae don't exist. The Stones aren't real. There is no power in love."

His father's cane whacked the chair. "By God, son, I have never raised a hand to ye, but ye sorely tempt me." He heaved a deep breath. "Yer foolishness with the Stone of Love was a costly mistake. A magical Iona Stone in the hands of the evil Fae doomed Scotland's battle for the crown. The battle of Culloden sealed our failure. Dagda claims it's at the hands of Balor, King of the evil Fae. Ye must do this!"

Alex yelled back. "Sacrifice and duty. Do ye know how hard it is being *The MacDougall* who ran away from a fight, Culloden, over his wife burning his feet?" He heaved a breath. "They call us cowards!"

His father leaned on his cane. "Dagda told me what would happen, that Balor saw to the end of the Jacobites to punish Scotland and us." His da beat his chest. "I *saved* our clan, and I would do so again!" He shook his head and spoke in a lower tone. "Now we are left playing tenant to the Campbells on my own damn property." He heaved a breath. "The whisky business saves us, and the promise of the tobacco trade will restore our wealth. But the Stone of Love ye must take back." Father and son stood panting, staring at each other.

The laird limped toward him and took him in an embrace. "I love ye with all my heart. Ye will do what is right, son." He held him momentarily, and Alex returned the embrace as tears built in his eyes. The lump in his throat prevented him from saying anything. With all they'd said over the years, what else was there left to say?

His father stepped back and patted his cheek. "I find

my rest now. Thankfully, yer dutiful housekeeper, Bertha, made up the guest room for me. I leave at sunrise." He turned and limped to the doorway.

When he arrived, he paused. "Think it over, son. Ye will find the way. We MacDougalls always do." The sound of his cane's uneven rhythm on the floor and then the stairs let Alex know his father had left him to his thoughts.

Alex stood staring into the fire's flames. To find the Stone of Love, one had to find love. Alex lost his sweetheart years ago, and the stone. He'd hardened his heart to romance, to love. They were a burden he was unwilling to take on again. An evil Fae took his sweetheart, and there was no way he'd find love.

He picked up the chest and carefully closed the clasp. He held the small trunk momentarily, the echoes of the stone's powers filtering into him. A glimmer of hope and faith washed over his heart. But the hard fact remained—love wasn't for Alex.

Crossing to the far side of the mantel, he bent to the bolt hole he'd placed there, just like at Dunstaffnage Castle. He opened the hide-e-hole and carefully set the chest inside. When his grip released the container, all hope and faith left him. He closed the bolt hole to the magic Iona Stones and his duty. Love was lost for him forever.

Chapter 2

Lady Iris Erskine strode through the streets of Glasgow, Scotland with purpose.

Her maid, Laurel Comyn, followed, carrying her daily purchases. "Mi'Lady, please, we must return to your home. 'Tis near dinner it is. Yer father will be home soon, and likely yer ma is worried sick." Her maid followed skipping to keep up. "Why ye taking the road by the slaughterhouse? It's the longest way home!"

Iris ignored her maid and confidante. She planned to slip past the meeting—just as she'd managed last week—to get to the secret Gaels gathering Laurel had mentioned. Not that Laurel's argument that most of the servants in her father's house were Scots deterred her. She wanted to see her Highlander in the outlawed plaid again. Maybe hear a bagpipe for the first time. She'd changed her path last week and walked past them, spying the most dashing Highlander in red, and she wanted to catch a glimpse of her Highlander again.

She sidestepped another rank puddle as she went down High Street toward the river Clyde and the slaughterhouse. The holiday decorations lit with candles, while pretty, didn't prevent her purpose.

Her mother's voice echoed from that morning. "An English jewel like you, Iris, should not worry herself with the Scots. You are a lady and should maintain decorum. Allow your maid to shop. We shall sit and take tea in the garden."

Iris groaned. She'd throw up if she had to sit through yet another boring tea with her mother's friends discussing the weather or the latest cloth at the merchant. However, Laurel's friend had the finest linen she'd ever seen.

Earlier, she'd stood in the shop as Laurel beamed at her friend Agnes, who had explained, "Weaved it myself from cotton from the Americas. Finest and tightest weave ye'd find in all Glasgow." The shop was actually the woman's home. Holly and ivy decorated the living room, where she'd spread out various textures and colors of the fine fabric.

Laurel nudged her friend. "Aye, and when Miss Iris tells all her friends where she got it, yer business will surely take off." Iris had to admit, the material was fine cloth. The reek from the slaughterhouse burned away her memory.

When she turned the corner of Bridge Street next to the pub, the stench hit her harder. She stopped, coughed, and turned toward the fresh scent of pine coming from the door's wreath. Her gaze connected with a man as he stood under the start of the bridge over the Clyde. A tall, striking man with jet-black hair leaned against the bridge's support pole. Many people mingled behind him, but when his gaze connected with Iris's she couldn't move if she wanted to. His electric blue eyes, the color of a clear sky, roamed her face. It was him, her Highlander!

She shifted her gaze, and for certain, he wore the same red tartan with green and blue threads running through it. The wind ruffled his shoulder-length hair. He still wore trews beneath his clan dress, but the image of bare knees, tanned and muscular, flashed in Iris's mind.

Laurel ran into her, breaking the connection. "Oh, miss. Why'd ye stop so suddenly? We are almost there, and ye clipped on at such a pace." Laurel bent to pick up the packages she dropped. As Iris stooped to help, her maid sighed. "Why, miss, ye did the same thing last week! Made me drop our purchases this time!" When Iris rose, the Scotsman's back was to her, but another in blue plaid stood before him.

The man in blue approached. "Laurel Comyn! Here, let me help ye with those." The man with a kind smile and walnut hair helped Laurel. The highlander in red disappeared into the crowd.

Her maid blushed as the man handed some packages to her and Iris. "Why, John MacArthur, thank ye kindly." He glanced her way, but his gaze went back to Laurel. Interesting. Iris didn't know Laurel had a beau.

His grin widened. "Will ye be joining us this evening? I missed ye last week." Laurel glanced at Iris, who smiled widely and nodded.

Laurel shook her head. "We can't, John, much as I want to. We must get these packages back for *the lady* of the house. She'd be spittin' mad if we were *late*." Iris didn't miss Laurel's emphasis on *lady* and *late*, but she wanted to speak to these people so badly.

John patted her arm. "Next week, then. I'll see ye here." He turned and strode into the crowd, who cheered a toast to whisky and Scotland. Next week, she'd be with them. She'd learn all she could about the man in the red plaid.

Laurel pulled on her arm. "Come along. We are late as it is. If ye dawdle any longer, I might find myself jobless and starving."

Arriving after dinner, Iris didn't have to explain their tardiness. It turned out that a fire on the riverfront delayed her father as well.

Now tucked into her bedroom, preparing for bed, Laurel shook out her dress. "Ye will not attend next week's meetin'. Why we barely made it home, and yer ma is right suspicious."

Iris picked up her latest find, a Gaelic poetry book, opened it, and tried to make out the words. "*Iain Gilpin. Iain Gilpin bha 'n a bhùir…*"

Laurel hung her dress up. "*Bha 'n a bhùirdeiseach.* Like *bush* and *ach* but roll ye r's." Iris rolled to her back, holding the book up as she mouthed the words.

Her maid pulled the covers back, tugging them from under her. "Ye got to know more than just saying the words. Ye got to know what they mean."

Iris rolled over and shoved her feet under the covers, secreting the book there. "You will help me? I must learn this in a week if I am to speak to the Gaels."

Laurel stopped and stared at her. "Is this why ye took the long way home these past two weeks just to walk past the meetin's?" She pointed a finger at her. "Ye will not come to a meetin'. Shame on me for encouraging ye like this. Yer ma will fire me for sure."

Iris sat up and grabbed her maid's hands. "Please, Laurel, I want to learn about your culture. I live here now and want to be a part of my father's work. To bridge the gap between our people."

Laurel shook her head as she patted her hand. "Aye, well, I suspect it has more to do with the man in the MacDougall plaid than anything else." She tucked Iris in. "I can't blame any woman for fawning over the likes of him. Alex MacDougall is a fine specimen of a man in a plaid." She fanned herself. "He makes all the women's knees weak." She glanced at her. "I allow ye one meetin', and that's it."

Iris grinned as her maid blew out the candles and left her alone. Then she rose from the bed, lit a taper, and crossed to light the candle by her bedside. Climbing in bed, she sat up and pulled her book from under the covers. She needed to do more than drink tea and speak of dresses and the weather. She had a sharp mind and a good heart. She'd win the Gaels over and be the Englishman to bring them into the modern era. Well, an English woman.

"*Bu mhòir a chliù, 's a ni.*" Was it *chlu* or *chli*?

The following day, Iris strode into the dining room late for breakfast. She yawned as she sat, and the maid served her tea—English tea.

She leaned over, whispering to their servant, "Did Cook get any of that black tea?"

The maid nodded and left as Iris's mother raised an eyebrow. "Black tea? Since when do you drink the Scots' tea?" Lady Jane Sterling Erskine was the epitome of an English woman, and while Iris loved her mother, she was sometimes a bore. Moving to Scotland had not gone over well with her mother, and the woman's attitude had become quite cumbersome.

Her mother called after the maid. "Make sure you ladies get the holiday décor up today. I want the place shining for the season."

Her father, Lord Erskine, huffed from behind his paper. "Leave the girl be. Scots' tea is actually quite good."

Iris shrugged as the maid returned with the tea. She dropped her dollop of cream in and took a sip, savoring the stronger taste.

Her mother sipped her tea, cleared her throat as she shifted toward her father. He startled and with a grunt, then scowled at her mother over the rim of the post. After spotting the frown her mother gave him, he folded the paper and sat up. Her mother had kicked him under the table again. Now, what did these two have in store for her? Last month, her event was a women's group that she'd found a total bore. What would her chosen project be this time? Maybe gardening? She liked to garden.

Her father cleared his throat. "Lieutenant Patrick Tytler of the queen's army and fifty-sixth brigade has asked permission to court you, Iris."

She tried to recall who on earth he meant. So many soldiers came and went from their home on her father's business. How each one eyed her like a fresh tart made her skin crawl. She wasn't a morsel for devouring, and based upon their expressions, she doubted any one of them had honorable intentions.

The one she despised the most flashed in her mind. She'd just returned from riding in the gardens at the university. In the stable yard a British soldier tried to bring his mount under control. He carried a whip and began beating his horse. The shrill of the animal's cries still haunted her, making her stomach turn.

She ran forward, grabbing his hand, only to have him shove her down. "Away from me, bitch. This animal doesn't know its master."

From the ground, she hotly replied, "A good master doesn't beat an animal into submission."

He'd raised his whip to her, and she covered her face. Instead of the expected sting of the lash, scuffling met her ears.

When she uncovered her eyes, the stable master had the officer by the arm. "'Tis Lady Iris ye address, Lieutenant. I suggest ye not whip the Lord's daughter."

Laurel had rushed forward and helped her up from the ground. "Come along, miss."

As she walked away, she glanced over her shoulder, and the Lieutenant's expression promised revenge. She shivered at the memory, hoping the officer in question was someone different.

Her mother nodded. "Lieutenant Tytler is an honorable man from an honorable family. I approve of the match."

Match? He only wanted to court her. Would her mother have her off and married before she'd even met the man? Didn't she have a say? This was seventeen fifty-three, not the medieval times.

She sat up. "I am not sure I am ready for callers. I barely know anyone here."

Her mother set her spoon aside. "Yes, and if you'd try to engage yourself with the proper parts of society, you'd meet more of your kind."

Iris glanced at her father, who rubbed his forehead. She gave him an expression she hoped showed her pleading with him. He hated her mother's parties, balls, and teas as much as she did.

He coughed. "Meet him once, Iris. If you don't like this man, maybe at the Hogmanay Ball your mother has planned, you will meet someone you like."

Her mother huffed. "I had hoped to announce…"

Her father stood speaking over her mother. "We have promised Iris the right to choose, Jane." He bent and kissed her mother's cheek as her gaze connected with hers across the table. That calculating gleam told

Iris this wasn't over by a long shot. Iris would have to be crafty to get past her mother. But maybe the mystery Lieutenant Tytler would be a dashing Highlander?

Later that afternoon, as Iris approached the terrace table where her mother and her friend, Mrs. Taft, sat with a British soldier, her hopes of a dashing gentleman vanished when he stood, and she came face to face with the very officer she hated with all her heart. She called him the horse beater.

Her mother beamed. "Iris darling, please let me introduce you to Lieutenant Tytler. Lieutenant or Patrick, this is my daughter, Iris." Her hands came to her middle as she stepped back.

He took her hand, which she'd not offered, and bent before it, kissing the back. "Charmed, my lady." His English accent clipped harder than her mother's. The edge to his tone was sharp. She'd grown accustomed to the rolling r's and s's of the Scots. Some English accents bothered her now. Chills shot down her spine, and when he rose, his smile tilted. Did he recall the confrontation in the stable yard as well? She pulled her hand from his and took the offered seat beside him.

Mrs. Taft poured her tea. "The lieutenant was just regaling us with his service to the King's army."

The officer took his cue well and beamed as he spoke. "Yes, I am here on service to keep the highlanders under the King's control. Any treasonous act will end with immediate and swift justice."

Mrs. Taft offered Iris cream, which she took with a shaking hand, poured a dollop, and set the creamer down.

Iris took a sip as the Lieutenant droned on. "I was fortunate to be part of the brigade at Culloden. Survived that battle unscathed and took many a Scot's life that day."

He sighed as Iris's tea got stuck in her throat. She coughed and managed to swallow it without spitting it across the table.

Mrs. Taft patted her back as she offered the plate of bread. "Scone, Iris?" Iris shook her head.

The Lieutenant leaned back in his chair. "Miss Erskine. Iris, if I may." She wanted to shout, *You may not!* But didn't in front of her mother.

She raised her gaze to meet his as the tilt returned to his smile. "Please do me the honor of riding with me in the college gardens later this week on Wednesday?" He bent forward as he grasped her hand, kissing the back. "It would bring me such pleasure."

Her mother moaned as Mrs. Taft giggled. Iris nearly threw up.

She pulled her hand from his. "I have plans."

Her mother blurted, "She'd love to."

Iris glared at her mother, who gave her a look Iris called *the eye* when she meant *do as you're told*. Iris sat back and plastered a fake smile on her face.

Her mother, *the great lady Jane*, in control and her element, beamed. "Lieutenant, please tell me of your pastime pleasures."

He sipped his tea and sat back again. "I love to train horses when I have the time. At my father's property in Kent, we have many horses. Some we breed for racing, and others we supply to the military." The image of him whipping the horse came to her mind, turning her stomach as he droned on. "To master the wild out of the animal, it's what I love. To tame them properly."

Mrs. Taft twittered, but for Iris, the only thing she heard was the sound of the horse's scream. The look on

Lieutenant Tytler's face, the joy he took in causing pain.

Unable to bear it any longer, Iris stood. "I am not feeling well." She stumbled away from the table.

The Lieutenant caught her before she could escape. "I am sorry, Iris. I didn't mean to disturb your delicate sensibilities."

She backed away, forcing him to drop his grip on her. "No, it's the air, it's turned sour." She turned and strode away, "Please excuse me."

Her mother spoke as she walked away. "Scotland hasn't agreed with her, and I must agree. You will come by at two on Wednesday?"

When Iris reached the doorway, she turned back. Lieutenant Tytler stood, flipped his coat tails behind him and bowed properly over his knee to Mrs. Taft, who fanned herself, and then to her mother. When he turned to leave, his eyes connected with hers. He nodded his head as if she was his next prey to master. Well, she wasn't a horse, and she sure as hell wouldn't be treated as one. It would be interesting to see what this ride on Wednesday would be like.

Chapter 3

Alex stood before Lord Erskine in what he considered his most important duty to the Scottish people. Officers had found William Harry with several stolen items in his and his wife's possession, but he claimed his tenant stole everything. Said tenant Elizabeth Richard spoke little to no English, only Gaelic, which was rare in this modern day but still found in some of the outer laying areas of growing cities like Glasgow and Edinburgh. Even though the language was outlawed, Lord Erskine had appointed Alex to take the woman's confession and interpret and read it in the case. She was due a fair trial regardless of the language she spoke.

He found her to be a kind and straightforward middle-aged woman during his time with Elizabeth. Having lost her husband at Culloden, she found herself at the mercy of those willing to offer charity for her to survive. It'd taken him two whole days, but here he stood, ready to deliver what he suspected would be a surprising testimony against William Harry.

Lord Erskine waved for Alex to begin. He glanced at William Harry, who wiped the sweat from his forehead and scowled at Elizabeth. This would certainly be interesting.

Before he began, he nodded to the Master at Arms as Alex took his agreed place near William Harry.

Alex would have no physical attacks in any

courtroom he oversaw. "Regarding the case against William Harry." He glanced at Elizabeth, who smiled at him. "The Confession of Elizabeth Richard taken before me, being one of his majesty's Justices of the peace in and for Glasgow, the first day of November seventeen hundred fifty-three."

He shifted his feet and leaned on the podium. "Mrs. Richard confessed that she robbed the house of widow Gwenllya Morgan four times. On two occasions, she stole some money, totaling three shillings. Once, she broke open a chest with a hatchet and took one piece of gold of the value of one guinea and twenty shillings in silver." He glanced at William, who sat grinning like a prized pig.

Well, this wasn't over—Alex had only begun. "Another time, she stole a box from Gwenllya Morgan's house. She broke it open in a field near the house, where she found seven silver shillings. Another time, she stole seven pence in halfpence out of another box in the house. Some other times, one linen cap, a handkerchief, an old, checkered apron, one linen shift, and one flannel shift. Also, she stole seven silver shillings from Barbara Howard."

Alex turned the page. Now, onto the real part of the confession. "She further confessed that William Harry encouraged her to go and rob their neighbors and that she carried all that she stole to him."

William stood and shouted. "I did not!"

Lord Erskine pounded his gavel. "Order!"

Alex continued after the ruling. "He harbored her in his house. She gave all she stole to William Harry. He claimed she had to do this for him to house her and pay for his new casting of bells and for the money for the corn to fatten his pig. The accused confided that the stolen linen shift she wore for some time and then gave it to William Harry's wife, who cut the shift to make a straining cloth to strain milk, then made the rest into caps for herself keeping the stolen items." From the gallery, William's wife gasped but said nothing else. William sat fuming, his face beet red.

Alex didn't pause. "William Harry also broke into Thomas John's barn. She claims he forced her to watch in the street while he stole barley out of the barn and that she held his mare ready in the lane to carry it off."

William stood again. "Lies, it's all lies!"

Alex didn't stop. "The accused claims that William Harry forced her to commit all the robberies. Yet, while she committed these crimes, his wife always advised her to be honest and not give herself up on stealing and pilfering. Even with his wife's preaching, William would fly in a passion and swear, curse, and abuse his wife." William lunged for Elizabeth, who jumped aside.

The Master at Arms grabbed William and held his arms behind his back as he yelled. "She's a whore, a no-good whore! Lies, all of it lies!"

The Justice pounded his gavel. "William Harry is found guilty of theft of all charges. A fine of twenty pounds levied against him."

William called out. "I haven't got twenty pounds!"

Lord Erskine leaned over his desk while he stared down at the room below. "Had you not spent all you stole, you would have. Make payment arrangements." He waved him away, and the officer dragged him from the courtroom.

Lord Erskine cleared his throat. "There are still the charges against Mrs. Richard."

Alex had prepared for this and discussed his recommendation with Elizabeth to ensure she was agreeable. "My lord, if I may suggest. While she is guilty of theft, she has no home, no way to make income but desires to serve this great city. May she give her penance in time served in the Hutchensone's Hospital and given residence there."

Lord Erskine nodded. "Wise choice, Alex." He swung his gavel. "Elizabeth Richard is guilty of theft and sentenced to service in the Hutchensone's Hospital and given residence there." Murmurs ran through the courtroom—the sentence was unique but a good choice.

Alex leaned down to Elizabeth. "*Tha e ag aontachadh. Bidh thu a' laighe agus ag obair aig Ospadal Hutchensone.*" He agrees. You live and work at Hutchensone's Hospital.

She patted his arm. "*Alex, tha thu nad thiodhlac bho Dhia. Beannachd leat agus chì mi thu aig a 'choinneimh.*" Alex, ye are a gift from God. Bless ye, and I'll see ye at the meetin'.

Alex grinned. Glad to have that one behind him, he looked forward to the rest of the day. The caseload was lighter. He hoped to find his rest at home soon.

****

Iris walked in from the garden, her gloves and apron covered in dirt. She loved to work there and be one with the land. It gave her such joy and relaxed her like nothing else.

Her mother spied on her from the parlor. "Iris dear. You must get ready for your ride with Patrick. He's due soon." She strode into the hall. "Why you've covered yourself in muck! Hurry, you must change."

Iris rolled her eyes. Was it Wednesday already?

Her mother screeched up the stairs. "Laurel! Laurel! Get Iris's riding dress and a basin of water." Jane waved her daughter to the stairs, and Iris trudged up, groaning. She should look on the bright side. She'd get to ride w*ithout* her mother, which meant galloping, and she planned to take advantage of it.

Not much later, primed and pressed, Iris stood with her mount in the stable yard awaiting Lieutenant Tytler. She patted Pixie, her mare, as she imagined today's ride would likely be a bore.

Lieutenant Tytler galloped into the small yard, and if Iris hadn't had a good grip on Pixie's reins, she might have bolted. Today, he rode a black Friesian stallion, rare yet beautiful. The horse pranced as the rider kept a firm grip on him. The stablemaster approached Iris and offered her a leg up. She accepted and easily mounted her favored mare.

Mac, the stablemaster, patted her leg as he murmured, "Miss, ye be careful. I don't trust the Lieutenant, and I hate that ye ride out alone with him."

Iris grinned and whispered back, "Well, if I am not back in the hour, send a rescue party. I don't plan to be in his company long."

Mac patted the horse as she rode to the *horse beater*. "Lieutenant Tytler, good day to you."

He bowed his head. "And to you, fine lady."

They walked their horses out onto the lane of Cambridge Street and turned left, heading toward High Street.

Iris nodded to the officer's horse. "Your horse is lovely. A Friesian stallion, most rare." As if sensing she discussed him, the horse shifted his head up and down, which meant he itched for a run. Good, so did Iris.

Lieutenant Tytler smiled as he held the reins tighter. "Ah, the lady is familiar with horses. I am impressed. Please call me Patrick." They maneuvered around a delivery cart as Patrick boasted, "He is mine, but not for long. He's here from my parents' stable under a contract of purchase from Lord Wellismere."

His horse sidestepped and skipped, but Patrick jerked the reins. "Ho, Caesar!" He held the spirited horse well, even if he had a heavy hand on the reins. "He needs a good run. Maybe I should run him while you walk." They turned left onto High Street, busier than Iris had ever seen. More wagons blocked the lanes as city workers hung holiday decorations. They planned to string evergreens from the candle street lights, the newest addition to Glasgow and something her father had raved about. He'd had a hand in their approval by the city improvement committee. She had to admit that as the greens went up, they gave the city a very festive look.

She smirked. "Nonsense, Lieutenant Tytler. Let's give them a trot to keep pace with the traffic." She'd used his title on purpose. The slight brought a frown from him, but she urged Pixie into a trot, cutting off more conversation as they headed down the lane toward Glasgow College and the gardens.

They both slowed to a walk again when they came upon the gardens. She gave Pixie a little of her head, allowing her to walk as she desired.

Lieutenant Tytler thankfully loosened his grip on Caesar's head, and the horse seemed to calm.

The Lieutenant was the first to break the silence. "Tell me, Iris, what do you like to do? Needlepoint, maybe?"

Iris had to laugh at that one. "No, I do not do needlepoint." She glanced at him, curious if her interests that weren't popular by society's standards for women would offend or interest him. His reaction would tell her a lot about him.

"I like to read. I do love not just poetry, but I also like to read Eliza Hollywood. *Love in Excess* is a favorite."

Lieutenant Tytler sat back. "The woman writer? I have not read her work."

The next one might certainly surprise him. "I like *Pamela* a lot."

The Lieutenant huffed. "Total rubbish. Why would you waste your time with that?"

Iris shrugged. "I liked it." They rounded a full bush of gardenias, reminding Iris of another of her hobbies. "I like to garden."

He chuckled. "My mother likes to garden. She gets her hands in the dirt and half over herself. Her roses are the most beautiful thing." So, gardening wasn't so bad to him, but what was he like as a person?

She leaned over. "So, Lieutenant. What do you like to do in your spare time?"

He sat up taller. "I like my duty, my work. It's honorable to bring civilization to the Scots."

She sniffed. "Civilized? I find them perfectly civilized. They just have different views than us. I don't find one more or less *civilized*."

Lieutenant Tytler tightened his hold on the reins. "Ms. Erskine, Iris, if you knew half the things I have seen in my duties, you wouldn't say that!" The sudden hardness of his voice gave her warning. His horse picked up on his rider's agitation and sidestepped, tossing his head. Iris glanced up at Observation Hill. It was a short gallop over the field to the river.

She tightened her reins. "How about a short run for your Caesar? I am certain Pixie is up for one as well." She nodded her head. "To the river and back?"

He grinned and nodded.

She didn't wait for him but kneed Pixie into a gallop, racing down the lane. Lieutenant Tytler and Caesar soon came up beside her. The Lieutenant held the reins tight, likely to keep pace with her smaller mare. As they hit the open field, Iris urged Pixie into a full-fledged run.

Lieutenant Tytler's burst of laughter carried to her, and he spurred Caesar into an open gallop that quickly overtook Pixie. Caesar was a magnificent animal and when allowed to stretch his legs, he quickly reached the river first.

As Iris came upon the Lieutenant, his tousled hair shifted in the breeze, and he held a boyish smile. "I hadn't had a run like that in ages." He blew a laugh as he looked years younger than the stern, formidable officer she'd seen in him.

He turned to her. "Thank you, Iris, that was quite refreshing." She bowed her head at his compliment. Not waiting, she nudged Pixie into a run.

Over her shoulder, she called, "Race you back!" They galloped back over the field, and when they reached the edge of the gardens, both slowed to a walk. Now, later in the day, people strolled, filling the park, not leaving them much room for anything other than walking the horses. Lieutenant Tytler stopped his mount, and Iris came beside him.

He leaned over and took her hand in his. "I have truly enjoyed today, Iris. Thank you." He kneed his mount, cuing him to sidestep so the horses bumped side by side, bringing the riders closer.

The Lieutenant's knee brushed hers as he held her hand firmly. "Your cheeks in the wind, they are like roses, Iris." Before she knew what he was about, he leaned over and brushed a kiss on her lips.

She yanked her hand from his. "Lieutenant Tytler, I haven't given you permission." Pushing Pixie into a trot, she nearly knocked aside a couple walking. She couldn't believe he took liberties without consent. She hadn't given permission to use her first name, let alone touch and kiss her. Ugh. Why were men like this?

She kept Pixie at a trot, intent on exiting the gardens to go home, with or without Lieutenant Tytler.

He came up beside her. "Iris, please. You spoke of the book *Pamela*. I thought that was an invitation." He glanced away, then back. "You must admit, from the prose in the book, mentioning it. Well, it seemed like an invitation."

Swallowing bile, Iris shivered. "It was not. I read— that's all."

Upon the exit, she nearly ran into a man entering, and when his head came up, it was him—the man from the Gaels meeting, the one who wore the red plaid.

Pixie chose that moment to shy, and Lieutenant Tytler took the reins. "Ho, I have her."

Caesar pranced around as the officer led both horses in a circle. The Lieutenant spoke, "Apologies, sir." When Iris came around, the man had moved away with his back to them.

Lieutenant Tytler maneuvered his mount to her side as they walked along. "You should heed your whereabouts and not allow your emotions to overtake you. But that's a typical woman's weakness." He rode ahead of her. "I'll take the lead so your mare will behave."

Behave, ha! *Woman's weakness*, not! Had he not taken liberties with her, she wouldn't have a reason to be so angry. Allowing the ride home to cool her *woman's weakness*, Iris vowed never to see Lieutenant Tytler again. His kiss was wet and slobbery, nothing like what she'd imagined a kiss from a man would be like. Not that she had anything in real life to compare it to, but still.

When they entered the yard, Mac came up to help her dismount. His familiar care helped cool Iris's nerves.

Lieutenant Tytler dismounted and came to her side as Mac took Pixie away. "An enlightening and enjoyable afternoon, Iris." He dipped his knee and bowed over his leg. "Thank you for the ride."

Iris only nodded as Lieutenant Tytler rose. He stood and gazed at her for a moment. She turned and gave him her back, hoping this was the last she'd see of him.

****

Alex strolled the gardens before heading home. They were a favorite respite during the years he'd studied and remained a place where he sought solitude and reflection. He didn't see the rider or the horse until the animal reared before him.

The British officer in full uniform grabbed the reins and turned the mount. The flustered woman on the mare was totally unaware of the dangers she placed them all in.

Alex continued his stroll after his near accident. He glanced over his shoulder and spied the light blue cloak of the female rider. Could it be the same woman? Certainly not.

He walked on. His father's letter troubled him. Another begging him to take on his duty to the stones, written in the code he liked to use, that started as a secret communication between him and his grandfather during the clan feuds that quickly turned into fond exchanges. When Alex was in college, his da sent them regularly to keep his spirit up, and they had. But this one wasn't meant that way. He pondered what it meant.

The lost lover can't pine for what he doesn't have.
To find love, one must open yer heart to it.
True love will bring the stone to life and to yer hand.
Yer duty is wasted, son, soon all will be lost.

He much preferred the ones that joked about law and life away from home to this one. How would Alex go about such an impossible task as retrieving a magic Fae stone? His da made it sound like his true love would cross his path and pop into his life. Love didn't work that way.

Chapter 4

Iris strode down the street beside her faithful maid, Laurel. "Miss, yer Gaelic is awful, and that accent."

Iris clipped her reply. "What of my accent?"

Laurel groaned. "It's English, very English. Ye'll stand out like a sair thumb among all the Gaels."

She wrapped the plaid, no *arisaid* tighter around her. "Sair, you mean sore?" She kept walking. "I am dressed like you. I can walk like you. I've un-styled my hair."

Laurel barked a laugh. "Ye walk like royalty, and no matter how much Gaelic ye learn, ye still sound like the Queen of England."

Iris stopped and turned to her maid. "I want to meet your people. Not because of the novelty." Laurel rolled her eyes, making Iris smile. "Well, *aye*, the novelty, but I want to learn the culture, about *yer* people."

Laurel's eyes crinkled. "Ye really want this, lass?" Iris nodded. Laurel took her arm in hers as they continued at a slower pace. "Then we need a plan, a canny one at that." She breathed. "Ye'll be my cousin. Ye wear the Comyn plaid, so ye'll be a Comyn. Stay beside me, and for all that is holy, don't speak. We'll say ye have a throat injury, so ye can't talk."

Iris stopped. "But what if I have a question or something to say?"

Laurel pulled her along the lane. "Ye don't have anything to say, and questions are for later. Just watch

and listen. *No talking*." They came up to the bridge—
many had already gathered as the slaughterhouse's smell
blew their way. Iris held her wrap to her nose, wondering
how they tolerated the stink.

A woman approached and took Laurel into a hug.
"So glad I am to see ye today." Laurel hugged her back.
"Mabina, glad I am to be here." She waved to Iris. "My
cousin, who is mmmm…"

Iris's eyes went wide. She didn't want to use her real
name and be found out before it was all over. She
panicked and glanced around. The pub beside the bridge
already had decorations for the holiday season, and holly
and ivy graced the doorway.

She pointed to the ivy, and Laurel grinned. "Ivy. Ivy
Comyn." She leaned over, whispering to Mabina, "She
doesn't talk, an old injury from a redcoat who tried to
have his way with her. Her throat don't work no more."

The woman tsked, "Sorry I am to hear it, Ivy." Iris
nodded as the plaid fell away from her head.

Mabina smiled. "Ye are a pretty thing, though."

The man in the blue plaid from last week
approached and took Laurel's hand. "Laurel Comyn, I
am happy to see ye this week." His regard drifted to her.
"And yer friend as well." His eyes went to her arisaid,
"A Comyn. She's yer…?"

Laurel shifted closer to him as she waved to Iris.
"John MacArthur, my cousin Ivy Comyn."

Mabina spoke from beside her. "She's mute, John.
Lost her voice." Iris nodded and moved her hand to her
throat.

A voice deep and rich called out over the crowd.
"Welcome all!"

Everyone turned and perched on a box he stood—

him, the man in the red plaid from last week. His deep black hair fell to his shoulders loose. As he raised his flask, his muscles undulated under the fabric of his shirt. Her focus traveled down, and today, he didn't wear trews under his plaid. Bare knees exposed above his woolen socks and boots fit for working on a farm were on his feet. Her knees became weak, and she reached out to Laurel as she stumbled.

Laurel took her hand. "First time ye seen bare knees, lassie? Does the same to me every time." When Iris's gaze returned to him, his eyes were on her.

He nodded her way and called out. "To whisky and Scotland!" The crowd repeated his toast, and everyone broke out in conversation.

Laurel turned to speak to John, leaving Iris beside the crowd. Many mingled and spoke lively. Men offered others sips from their flasks as the women huddled together, gossiping about whatnot. Iris picked up a Gaelic word here and there. *Taigh* for house and *bonnach* for bannock. She enjoyed the rich brogue of the men's voices and the rolling of the r's in the women. Their outspoken banter brought a smile to her face.

A gust of wind blew through the area, clearing the slaughterhouse stench but brought on a chill. Iris went to cover her head, and her arisaid fell on one side.

"Here, lassie, allow me." His rich baritone voice sent chills down her spine, and as she turned, she came face to face with—him.

He'd caught her plaid and wrapped it around her body, tucking it into the folds so it stayed put in the breeze. "My ma taught me the simple fold to keep her plaid in place." His hand lingered on the fabric near her face. "Comyn, ye are a Comyn, like my ma."

She swallowed and shivered again, but not from the cold. The light blue of his eyes lit up the night as they followed hers. She glanced down again, unsure what to do without a voice to converse with.

When her face rose, his eyes crinkled. "Have I scared ye lass?" His hand dropped, and he blew his breath. "I didn't mean to." She stared at him, a highlander she craved to be near, her highlander. He cleared his throat. He'd asked her something. Iris shook her head, her hand going to her throat. She opened her mouth, and nothing came out but air, hoping to get her point across.

Her Highlander's eyebrows rose. "Ye can't speak?" Iris shook her head.

His smile bent kind of sideways. "I am Alex, Alex MacDougall." He took her hand in his and caressed it. "What shall I call ye then?"

Iris's focus went to the greenery décor, and he followed. "Holly?" She shook her head, her gaze never leaving his.

He grinned. "Ivy then?"

She nodded as his thumb brushed the back of her hand, and he stepped closer. "Did you know ivy is also called *lovestone* due to its tendency to grow over bricks and stones? Ivy clings to any surface, making it a perfect representation of love and fidelity."

Iris's face warmed. With her other hand, she pointed to the holly plant, then pulled her hand from his and made the sign of the cross.

As his eyes followed her actions, he spoke. "The holly is a sign of Christ."

She nodded vigorously. That's how she could speak with him—mimicking her words. She pointed to the ivy, waved her hands around her arisaid wrap on her head, and gave him a humble expression.

He chuckled. "The ivy is the virgin, Mary. Aye, I have heard this as well." The cold wind blew harder, and she brought her hands to her mouth, blowing on them to keep them warm.

Her highlander took her hands in his. "Come, lass, let's get ye out of this wind and by a fire." He led her into the crowd.

Many stopped them as he wove his way through people. "Oh, Alex, no speech tonight? No guiding words from our leader?"

He shook his head. "No, just good company tonight, James."

An older woman stopped him. "Heard what ye did today for Elizabeth Richard. Right kind of ye." She patted his arm. He nodded as he pulled Iris to the brazier, rubbing her arms. She glanced back at him. Her hands came up, and she made the shape of a crown, then pointed to him as she tilted her head to the side.

He stopped his rubbing. "Are ye asking if I am the King?" He blew a laugh. "No, not the bloody King of England." She smiled and shook her head. She waved around, then pointed to him and repeated the crown sign.

He nodded. "Ah, leader? Aye, I am the leader of sorts, ye could say. The Gaelic people look to me for advice, that's all." Iris glanced back at the older woman who'd stopped them before, then back at him. She pointed at the woman, then to him, and raised both hands in question.

His gaze followed her movements. "Ye ask what I did today?" He blushed and glanced down. "Nothing that isn't my job." She grabbed his hand and took it as she stepped forward, tilting her head to the side.

Her highlander stared into her eyes for a moment, then sighed. "I saved a woman from being wrongly accused. She couldn't speak much English. Her landlord had accused her of theft, but he took advantage of her and forced her to commit the crimes." He glanced away, then back at her. "Ye could say I *thug e dha*."

She stared blankly at him—she'd not encountered those words yet.

His eyebrows rose. "Not much Gaelic in ye lass? I *gave it to him*. I interpreted her confession for her that placed the blame on him."

Iris nodded, understanding now, glad Laurel had convinced her not to speak. Her accent was bad enough, but trying to understand the Gaelic was too much to get anyone there to believe she was a Scot. Yet, she'd found a way to communicate anyway.

Laurel and John came up beside them as others filtered away. She'd not noticed that the crowd had thinned, and the night had grown later.

Laurel took her arm in hers. "Alex, I see ye have met my cousin, Ivy." She pulled her away. " 'Tis late, Ivy. The *missus* would be in a fit if we arrived late *home*." Iris pulled back, not wanting to leave.

Her highlander's focus moved between them. "Ye serve with Laurel at Lord Erskine's home?" Iris glanced at Laurel. He'd discovered her lie!

Laurel smiled. "Aye, Alex, she does. Part-time." Laurel's eyes met hers. "And we must leave soon." Laurel pulled her away as her eyes connected with Alex.

He stepped forward, taking her hand. "Luncheon with me tomorrow? At Mabina's High Tea Room on Argyle Street. Noon, please?"

Iris's panicked expression flew to Laurel's, who pulled her along. "I don't think she has the time, Mi'Laird." Iris shook her head and pulled out of Laurel's grasp. She went to Alex and took his hands in hers as she nodded.

He bent and kissed her hands. "I will look forward to our meeting, Ivy."

John called out after Laurel. "Why don't ye join us, me as well?"

This made Laurel draw up. "John MacArthur, are ye askin' me to dine?"

He grinned. "I think I just did."

Her highlander smiled. "Then tomorrow it is."

Iris stared as Laurel pulled her away. She kept her eyes on Alex as he stood under the bridge, watching her depart. Her heart rose in her chest, and her stomach fluttered. Her hand still tingled from his kiss.

Laurel muttered as they walked away. "Sneaking away again. I'm to be fired for sure, but to get time with John, finally,"— she fanned herself—" 'Twas worth it!"

****

Alex stood rooted in the same spot as her cousin pulled away the auburn-haired beauty. Ivy, her name was Ivy. And she was a Comyn. Strange last week when he'd seen her leading Laurel, who carried packages. He could have sworn he had the impression she was a lady and Laurel, her servant, not cousin.

She turned the corner, and John punched his arm. "The auburn-haired lass turned yer fancy anyway, eh?" Alex chuckled, not commenting. He turned to retrieve their horses from Jimmy, who stood in the cold patiently waiting.

Alex handed him two shillings. "See that yer ma

gets better, Jimmy." He took it with a grin. It was twice the amount Alex typically tipped him for looking after their horses.

Both men mounted and took off in a trot for home. They turned up on High Street. With the lampposts lit and the newly decorated greenery combined with the candles burning, lighting the wreaths on the doors, a festive feeling flooded Alex with nostalgia, making him miss home. His ma loved to decorate for the holidays, and few could decorate like her.

Glasgow had grown into quite a modern town with the new planning in place. The city planning office had approved and started relaying the roads into a grid, like Edinburgh. They had ordered most of the buildings built with stone not wood. No thatch roofs were permitted— stone and shingles slowly replaced the wood and thatch. His townhome, being newly built, fell within the regulations.

John came up beside him. "So, Ivy Comyn, eh?" They turned onto Ingram Street, which was before the college. At the end of the row, the new townhomes sat. Alex didn't answer John's inquiry, knowing he referred to his comment last week about not wanting to find love.

Unable to let it rest, John spoke again. "A lovely creature, isn't she? And a Comyn to boot."

They rode into the stable yard behind the houses. Each homeowner contributed to the whole of the stable to house their horses and other livestock. A convenient consolidation of resources that worked well for them. It housed cows for milk, chickens for eggs and cooking, hogs, and other livestock and horses. There was practically a whole farm in his backyard.

He dismounted and handed his horse to Will, the

stablemaster. John did the same, thanking him. Alex ran up the back steps and into his town home. His post sat on the entry table, and he flipped through it as John entered.

Alex held up a letter. "Another from my da." He threw it down.

John came up beside him. "Ye aren't going to read it?" He chuckled. "I at least like to see how creative he can be when wording yer duty to the stones."

Alex waved to the letter as he strode into the parlor and poured himself a dram. "Ye read it then."

John picked up the letter, broke the seal, and read aloud as he followed. Alex sipped his whisky as John's words echoed in the dark room lit by the lone fireplace.

A fable has shown itself.

A prince and false love found true in a maiden by a stream.

A maiden's sacrifice.

Only through love will ye find the way, laddie.

Yer time is upon ye.

As John finished reading, Alex gulped the rest.

John handed the parchment to him then he poured himself a whisky. "The *Fae Fable Book* has shown a tale. A stone ye must find." He grumbled, "At least that's what my da Archibald MacArthur claims."

Alex sat before the fire, staring at his da's letter. "I've never seen the book change. I wonder how it does it being in the case and all."

John sat in the chair beside him. "Do ye recall when they first sat us down telling us about the Fae, the book, and our duty?"

Alex snorted. "Aye. Stories were all they were. A heart stone for love with a maiden. A blue diamond for faith and the island that sank with a maiden calling for her true love to save her. That tale is not in a book but told by a distant relative."

John gazed into the fire as he twirled his glass. "The green stone for hope, broken by two jealous siblings only to have the son find it whole in another faraway land."

Alex sat staring into the flames. "I didn't believe it. Not until my ma opened her locket and the Stone of Love glowed." His eyes teared. "When she described what the stone made her feel. Her love, combined with my da's, I was so overwhelmed." His throat closed, making his voice waver. "Their love, so strong and powerful." He looked at the letter again and whispered, "True love is the greatest power of all." He recalled Ivy nodding to the holiday décor. Ivy, love stone. Was it a sign?

He sat back. "God, John, I worry. When I first locked eyes with Ivy a week ago, I felt it. That *bolt* my ma and da speak of. Yer parents too. The jolt to yer heart upon seeing yer true love for the first time." He sat forward, set his glass on the table, and ran his hand through his hair. "How will we do it, John?"

John sat forward and patted him on the shoulder. "Like we always have for generations, together."

Alex nodded. "Aye, but if the Stone of Love fable has shown itself and the Stone of Love is what we must seek, then is Ivy the maiden?" His gaze met his closest ally and friend for his whole life. "She will sacrifice herself for the stone, no matter what I do. Like Heather."

John gulped his whisky and stood. "My da said that Colin MacDougall from the future claimed the stories were a guide, not a literal translation. So, maybe it's a metaphor? Either way, we'll get through this, Alex. Ye said ye have the two stones, Faith and Hope, in the brooch. We'll use them when the time comes."

Alex breathed. "Have faith and hope, aye."

Chapter 5

Lord Erskine set aside the stack of papers. "Well, that's it for the review of cases for this morning." He sighed as he faced Alex from across his desk. "Luncheon with me, Alex?"

Alex stood. "Sorry, my lord. I have plans."

His friend blew a laugh, "Plans again? Alex, my boy, it must be a woman!"

Alex's face heated as he took the stack of papers and handed them to the filing clerk. "A gentleman doesn't speak of his activities with women, my lord."

Lord Erskine puffed. "Right, you are Alex. Did you get the invite to the costumed masked ball for Hogmanay? Speaking of women, my wife was quite adamant you join us."

Alex stood and nodded. "Aye, I'll be there, but not sure of the costume."

Lord Erskine laughed. "You are the toast of the town. The Highlander who's bridged the gap and made life easier for us all together." He leaned toward him and winked. "Wouldn't it be grand if you showed up dressed fully in your plaid?"

Alex grinned at the image James made. It would be scandalous and a hoot. "Wait, my lord, plaids are outlawed."

Lord Erskine called over his shoulder as he exited the room. "If you have a bagpipe, bring it. What a spectacle."

****

Iris and Laurel arrived at the High Tea Room to the full crush of the luncheon crowd. Iris had loaned one of her day dresses to Laurel so both would blend in better in the noontide throng, but she didn't really need it. The High Tea Room was one of the few growing establishments that didn't insist on class and rank. Mabina McGee refused to allow the British to dictate anything more than the written law when it came to how she ran her tearoom. Iris loved it. It's funny how the way through some staunch societal rules was through the belly.

Outside the front door, Iris giggled until her father's stern voice rose behind her. "Hi and ho, Lord Willismere! Luncheon with me. I heard of your newly acquired horseflesh. Join me and tell me of it."

Iris's eyes widened as she turned to Laurel, who twisted toward her, her mouth open.

Laurel grabbed her hand, dodged some patrons and took off down the alleyway. "The back door, it's the only way not to be spotted by yer father."

Iris pulled on her hand. "But the men, Alex and John. Don't they wait in the front?" They ran down the alley, rounded the corner, and thankfully, the back door stood open.

Laurel poked her head into the kitchen. "Mabina! Mabina!" The cook and a scullery boy turned as both women entered and strode through the kitchens

Mabina burst through the doorway and nearly ran Laurel over. "Laurel, what are ye doing in my kitchens?" She eyed Iris, and a smile spread on her face. "Meetin' anyone, ladies?"

Iris open her mouth, then shut it with a click of her teeth. She'd almost replied to the Scot.

Laurel brushed her hands down the front of her gown. "Aye, and the crush up front has made us tardy. Is John MacArthur here yet?"

Mabina's grin grew wider if that was possible. "Aye, in the back room. He asked for a more private table he did. Arrived before the rush." She moved past them, setting down her tray of soiled dishes. "Alex MacDougall hasn't arrived yet, but John says he's on his way." She eyed Iris. "Ivy, is it?" Iris nodded as Mabina led them through the dining room that Mabina had decorated for the holiday season. Evergreens and mistletoe covered nearly every surface. The green pine scent was magical. Mabina walked on and directly past her father.

Iris ducked her head and quickly turned the corner after Mabina, who cut in front of Laurel as her father's voice rang out. "Laurel, what are you doing here?" Laurel stopped, but Iris kept walking to the back, not turning. She ducked behind a pillar. The evergreens helped keep her hidden as she spied on her father and maid as they spoke.

Laurel stopped, took Lord Erskine's arm, and turned him where his gaze was to the front of the dining room. "I am meeting a friend. After, I am to run errands for Iris, Mi'Lord."

Her father nodded as Lord Willismere waited for him.

He turned to join his friend as he waved to Laurel. "Good. Be a good girl and stop by the cigar shop to pick up my package on the way."

Laurel nodded. "Aye, Mi'Lord." When her father

passed Laurel, Iris sighed, and her shoulders sagged. Laurel's expression was one of anger, then shock. Someone from behind tickled Iris, and she had to close her hand over her mouth to cut off a yelp.

Iris turned, and Alex held her in his arms. "Ivy. Spying on people, should I have ye hauled in?" Iris' heart nearly lurched from her chest. She slapped the arms that encircled her and held her steady.

Laurel approached and took her arm, forcing Alex to release her. "Come, *Ivy*, let's join the men for lunch." Alex followed as he chuckled.

As they approached John, his friend grinned and stood for Laurel. Iris sat as Alex held the chair for her. The menus were out, and they quickly ordered from the servant boy. John and Laurel spoke lowly between themselves as Iris picked at her napkin. The boy set the drinks down, all ale, and soon Mabina set their dishes before them.

Alex had a meat pie, John the Cullen Skink soup with fresh bread. Laurel opted for the baked sliced Grosse with tatties, and Iris had the salmon with steamed crab. Seafood was her favorite, and the fare of Scotland far beat London's. If she could, she'd eat fish daily. Her mother preferred boiled beef. The rough texture and heavy sauces turned Iris's pallet. When Iris forked her first flaky bite, she moaned a little in her mouth. Alex froze and stared at her.

Laurel lifted her head. "Ivy can make some noises, but it's rare. She's embarrassed by them. They aren't commonly." Iris bent her head down and set her fork on the plate.

She reached for her ale, and Alex's hand reached for hers. "Ivy."

She jerked her gaze up, and their eyes connected. "Any sound ye make is heavenly because it's yer voice. Please don't hold back in my presence, ever." He lifted her hand to his and kissed the back then rubbed the spot with his thumb as he smiled. Alex released her hand near her ale and continued with his meal.

Ivy picked up her cup with a shaky hand and drank deeply. Alex's kisses sent tingles up her arm and down her spine. When she had a hard time cracking her crab, he wordlessly took them, cracked her crab for her, and set the lumps on her plate, smiling when she gobbled them up. His demeanor warmed her, and she quickly became comfortable with him.

Alex sat back after finishing. "Ivy, Laurel mentioned ye work part-time with her at Lord Erskine's home. Is that where I may send messages to ye?"

Her gaze caught Laurel's, who sputtered. "Alex, ye should send them to me. Ivy isn't always at the manor house." Iris nodded. That sounded like a good explanation. Certainly, if messages to a servant who wasn't in their employ suddenly showed up, her ever-controlling mother would soon get to the bottom of any mystery.

Mabina passed by after the servant cleared their dishes. "Cruachan, anyone? Freshly made. Last of the raspberries for the season." She patted Alex's shoulder. "Even made with the MacDougall whisky." Iris sat up, her gaze pleading with Alex.

He nodded to Mabina. "We'd love some."

She touched his arm and nodded to the table. Alex patted her hand and turned to speak to John. Iris wanted to know about this whisky from his family. Her father loved whisky, and she often snuck some without her mother knowing. Whisky was a favorite of hers.

Iris tapped his arm again, and he waved her off. She exchanged a glance with Laurel, who hid her giggle in her napkin. Iris eyed John, who hid his smile in his hand. Alex kept his back to her. She hit the table, and the remaining dishes clattered.

Alex slowly turned to her with a wide grin. "Something ye wish to ask, dearie?"

She made the shape of a whisky bottle with her hands and mimicked pouring and taking a shot, then pointed at him. He watched her hands as they moved fast, her frustration building.

Alex chuckled, "Ivy, are ye telling me ye like the drink?" She loved whisky. If his family had a label, she'd love to try it. Granted, she'd never bothered to look at her father's labels, but she would now.

She stared at Laurel, who hid her laughs into her napkin. "Ivy likes a nip every so often." Iris stuck her hand out, counting on her fingers, all of them.

Alex and John burst out laughing as Alex spoke, "Ye like a dram all the days, Ivy?" Ivy nodded, pointed to him, then to her, and motioned to drink again. Mabina set the desserts in front of them as Ivy kept eye contact with Alex, demanding an answer.

He bowed his head. "The lady's wish is my command. Mabina, bring a shot for us all of my family's label, The Heart of Scotland."

Iris nodded and smiled as Alex pointed at her dessert. "Eat yer sweet, dearie. The berries, cream, and oats will make the taste of the whisky better."

She dug her spoon into the familiar mixture of raspberries, cream, and oats. The first bite was heaven, sweet and creamy. When she swallowed, the nip of the liquor hit her tongue. She had to concentrate to not moan again. She had another bite and another as Alex chuckled next to her.

Soon, a snifter sat beside her. She eyed Alex, who nodded to the drink. As he sipped his, she picked the glass up, stuck her nose into it, and sniffed. Rich wooden tones hit her nose with a hint of the nip. Her eyes connected with Alex's. Her father had this brand. This one was his favorite. She took a sip and held the liquor in her mouth, allowing the flavor to settle, then swallowed.

Alex hummed. "She does know how to drink it right." He turned to Laurel. "Best make sure ye walk her home, though."

Iris offered the drink to him, insisting he have the rest. He took the glass and eyed her over the rim. He turned the snifter to where her lips had drunk from and locked his on the glass. He kept them there for a moment, not drinking. He inhaled, closed his eyes, and drank the rest in one gulp.

Alex set the glass down and leveled his gaze upon her. "Heavenly." His reaction nearly had Iris melting in her chair. Had she been standing, her knees would have buckled.

He stared at her as John rose. "Ladies, it has been lovely, but Alex, ye must get back to the courthouse. Cases."

Alex stood, took Iris's hand, and kissed the back. "It was a pleasure."

Mabina strode by, and Alex stopped her. "Send the bill over. As usual, the food was delicious."

He walked around Ivy and bent to whisper in her ear. "Till next time, Ivy. And I'll bring the whisky." He brushed a kiss on her neck and sauntered out the door with John following.

Her face swung to Laurel, and she mouthed, *oh my* as her entire body shivered. Alex was more than she bargained for and everything in between.

Laurel smiled. "I think we'll be having more outings, Ivy." The only response Iris could manage was a nod.

****

The following morning, her bed curtains opened with a jerk. "Laurel, leave me be. I wish to sleep in."

She rolled over as the sound of her mother's humming filled the room. Lord, what now? Her mother, happy and humming early in the morning, only meant one thing. She'd planned something for Iris, and the plans usually ended up being something Iris hated. Her mother laid her day dress on the bed. She rolled over, and Laurel stood by the doorway with the stable boy hauling in the hip bath.

Iris sat up. "Mother, you don't have to make them haul that thing up the stairs. I can bathe in the kitchens."

Jane Erskine turned to her. "Nonsense. Today is a special day." She returned to the armoire and flipped through more of Iris's dresses.

Iris caught Laurel's eyes and mouthed, *What now?*

Laurel mimicked eating as another boy hauled in water. Her maid glanced at her mother, and Iris's gaze followed. She still rifled through her dresses, not noticing their exchange.

Her gaze swung back to Laurel, who stood tall and saluted her. Damn, dinner with the Lieutenant. She didn't like the man, and now that she'd met and gotten to know Alex MacDougall, there was no one else she wanted to spend time with. Her mind scrambled for an excuse to bow out. Ill, she'd plead ill.

She lay back in bed, moaning. "Oh, I feel awful."

Her mother turned. "Nonsense. A bath and some hot tea will fix you right up." She held up one of Iris's best dresses. "We are hosting Lieutenant Tytler, Mrs. Taft, and her husband for dinner." She held the dress out to Laurel. "Have this pressed. Bathe and dress her in her best. Dinner is at six." As she marched out the door, she called over her shoulder, "Stay out of the whisky, Iris. Ladies don't drink strong spirits."

****

Promptly at six in the evening, the doorbell sounded throughout the house. Iris and Laurel hid at the top of the stairs.

Iris turned to her trusted friend. "I can't stand the man. A whole dinner with him? Why?"

Laurel shook her head. "Ye don't want to know, Iris."

Iris tugged on her friend's arm. "Tell me."

Her confidante sighed. "Yer mother wants ye to marry Lieutenant Tytler." Iris's eyes went wide.

Her maid put her hand out. "Yer da, he argued it's yer choice. Like he's promised. They've argued for days." She bowed her head. "Please don't say anything. I wasn't to tell ye."

Iris took her best friend's hand in hers. "I would never betray you. But what to do of my mother's trickery."

Laurel smiled. "Yer da, he's the answer. Convince him ye hate the gadgie and let him deal with the crabbit woman." Iris giggled. Her mother could be crabbit at times.

As the guests arrived, Iris and Laurel stayed at the top of the stairs. Mrs. Taft's lively laughter carried upward as her husband's jovial voice echoed, "I do hope you have a spread ready to feed the King. I am famished."

Mrs. Taft replied through her puffs. "And he'll eat as much as the King as well." Their voices died down as they moved into the parlor.

The bell rang again, and the door opened. The officer's voice clipped loudly. "Lieutenant Tytler for dinner." He'd made the announcement as if he reported for duty. And likely, that's how he viewed this evening. She hated tonight already.

Her mother's voice drifted up. "I wonder where Iris is. The guests have arrived."

"I'll get her, you see to your guests." His heavy footfalls came up the stairs.

Iris turned to Laurel. "Here goes nothing."

She started down the stairs. At the turn, she encountered her father, smiling as he held his whisky glass. "Ah, there you are." He took a sip and whispered, "Ready for another of your mother's dinners?"

Iris sighed. "No, and why the Lieutenant?"

Her father eyed her. "Don't you like Patrick?" Iris stared him straight in the eye and shook her head.

He took another sip and then exhaled. "Try to get to know him, Iris. He's a well-respected officer." Iris huffed.

Her father handed her the glass. "Have one nip before you face the matchmakers in action." She took the glass, had a sip, then another.

He grabbed at the glass. "Not too much. If your mother smells liquor on you I'm done for." Iris rolled her eyes and handed her father back the glass as she stepped past him to move down the stairs. The evergreen garland on the stairway covered most of the railing. Iris placed her hand in the open spaces.

She moved into the parlor, and Lieutenant Tytler decked in his uniform stood by the evergreen covered fireplace, with his arm resting on the mantel, holding a glass. He made the picture of a perfect British officer. Mr. Taft stood beside him, and her mother and Mrs. Taft sat in the settee with their heads bent together, twittering like two little birds.

Her father followed her into the room. "Here she is."

Lieutenant Tytler lifted his head, and a wide smile graced his face as he sauntered to her. He stepped back, formally bowed over his front leg and offered his hand to take hers.

She glanced at her father, who nodded to the Lieutenant. As he rose, she offered her hand.

The Lieutenant grabbed her and kissed the back. "My Lady. Iris, you look lovely this evening."

She smirked. "You as well." He released her hand and took a sip of his drink.

Brandy wafted to her nose as he slid closer. "Please call me Patrick, Iris. I think we are familiar enough now." She stiffened.

Her mother rose. "Dinner is ready. Let's all move into the dining room. She flitted out as she called over her shoulder, "I have a delightful meal planned." Mrs. Taft rose and followed. Lieutenant Tytler waved ahead of him. When she stepped before him, he placed his hand at her lower back. She jolted from the unexpected contact and walked faster into the dining room.

Behind her, her father spoke to Lieutenant Tytler.

"So, how is your post here in Scotland going, Patrick?"

His voice rose slightly behind her, "Well, my lord."

Her mother stood at the head of the dining table, tall and proud, with a wide smile as the table overflowed with evergreens laced with holly and ivy, reminding Iris of Alex. Would she ever look at ivy the same again? She doubted it.

Her mother's voice interrupted her musings. "The Tafts, please sit on my left." She indicated the two chairs on that side of the table. "Lieutenant Tytler, Patrick. Please sit beside me." She waved to her right. "Iris, your place is beside Patrick." Her place was never beside that man but she moved there anyway. She breathed deeply telling herself, a scene in front of her mother was worse than a dinner next to the *horse beater*.

Lieutenant Tytler held her chair out for her, and when she sat, he set his hands on her shoulders, making her stiffen. Her gaze connected with her father's, who eyed the Lieutenant's hands as his expression shifted to a scowl. Her mother sat and waved to the servant, who brought out plates filled with sliced roast beef, potatoes, and peas, all soaked in a rich gravy. Another servant rounded the table, filling the wine glasses with a deep red wine.

As the meal progressed around Iris, conversations of manly endeavors went back and forth with an occasional joke from Mr. Taft. The latest tobacco or a new mount, things that would be the talk at the local pub. They almost sounded like women gossiping, the newest tea, a newly arrived fabric at the milliners, and the latest scandal mentioned over tea. The women, as usual, sat not commenting, and for the first time, the societal requirement for a woman to not speak sat well with her while the meal didn't. She forked another bite of rough, overcooked beef as she allowed the thick gravy to drip off. She'd finished the peas and the potatoes she'd fished from the gravy, hoping the drippings would fill her. As she tried to swallow the dry meat, she picked up her wine glass, took a large sip, and the piece went down, tasting better in the rich red wine. Her mother's scrutiny focused on Iris as she raised an eyebrow. Not caring what her mother thought, she took another deep gulp.

Her father's strong voice drowned out her mother's huff. "Lieutenant Tytler, I understand you had a rather interesting case the other day."

The officer set his fork down. "I had to attend the coroner's view of the body of Edward Kemeys outside of town. John Rimbron employed him to carry stones uphill to a limekiln. The stupid Scot fell into the said limekiln, which was on fire. With the sulfur and smoke, he suffocated and instantly died."

Mr. Taft coughed. "Sounds ghastly if you ask me." Mrs. Taft gagged and took a sip of her wine.

The scent of sulfur and smoke wafted to Iris' nose even though they sat in her dining room. The thought of the death turned her stomach as she set her fork down, but the insult to the man?

She turned to Lieutenant Tytler. "What does him being a Scot have to do with his falling into the pit?"

Tytler sat taller. "Scots are known as lazy, careless, and drunkards. I suspect he was inebriated at the time. A just death."

Iris's mouth fell open. He didn't just call the Scottish people lazy, careless, and drunkards. Her gaze roamed to the footman by the door, who glared daggers at the man. Iris felt the same.

Her father spoke quickly, his firm voice carrying an edge. "Wasn't he overcome with the sulfur, Lieutenant Tytler, not the drink?" He picked up his wine glass and swirled it. "Something any common man could succumb to—English or Scot."

The officer snorted, "I am convinced it was the drink. But the coroner has the body and will determine the cause of death." Iris shivered. The thought of a body left in the hospital, cold and alone, made her want to curl up and have her father hug her.

Her father leveled his glare on the Lieutenant. "Of that, I am sure." Her eyes met her father's, who glared at the man. She'd seen that look before. Lieutenant Tytler should heed the warning. Her father was angry.

Lieutenant Tytler picked up his wine glass, sipped, and sighed. "I heard of the scene in your courtroom the other day. Why you allowed that outlawed barbaric language to be spoken is beyond me."

Her father waved his hand. "I had to. They'd accused the poor woman unlawfully. She had rights, and Alex MacDougall had to step in since she couldn't speak anything but Gaelic." This caught Iris's attention, and her head snapped up. Alex, they spoke of Alex. She set her glass down.

Lieutenant Tytler cleared his throat. "Well, if you ask me, Alex should be arrested."

Her father laughed. "For following my orders? I think not."

The lieutenant slammed his glass down. "The Gaelic language is outlawed."

Her father spoke low, his tone broking no argument. "Maybe, but the Scots still speak what they know. There is no harm in their culture as long as they do as the King bids. Most of them only try to make a living. Live to the next day, *like us all*."

Iris couldn't resist commenting. "I like the Gaelic language. I find its cadence like a song. Soulful and beautiful." Lieutenant Tytler sat back, staring at her. She didn't turn but spotted his stunned expression from the corner of her eye. Let him be shocked. Maybe he'd leave her alone if he knew she liked Scottish people.

Her mother's fork clanked when she dropped it. "When have you heard Gaelic? Oh, it must be the servants." She glared at her father. "I told you moving here would ruin her." Iris's eye caught the footman rolling his eyes. When he saw Iris staring, he winked at her.

Her father exhaled. "Learning new customs has not ruined anyone. I enjoy learning about the Scots, and Alex has been key in helping my work here." Her father's gaze caught hers. "We've invited him to the masked ball for Hogmanay." He winked at her. Iris grinned as she dropped her focus to her lap. Was she that transparent?

Lieutenant Tytler cleared his throat. "I got the invite and look forward to the grand ball." He picked up Iris's hand. She pulled away, but he held it. "Iris will honor me as my escort." His other hand lifted his glass toasting everyone. "We shall all ring in the New Year together."

Her mother took hers and toasted with them. "To the New Year."

Iris didn't join the toast. The last thing she wanted was to celebrate this moment. This was nothing like the fun, exciting luncheon she'd had yesterday—an enjoyable, comfortable exchange between her, Alex, Laurel, and John. Friends enjoying a good meal together. She blew out her breath. Even without her voice, she'd communicated so much more to Alex and he to her than the exchanges she'd had the entire evening with the Lieutenant. He barely knew her but sat there holding her hand like she was his possession.

Her mother nodded to the footman, who opened the dining room doors as she turned to speak to Iris. "I arranged for you and Lieutenant Tytler to share dessert in the parlor. Your maid shall sit with you for propriety."

Lieutenant Tytler stood as he held her hand practically dragging her from the table. Struggling to stand, Iris grabbed her wine glass. When they arrived in the parlor, he led her to the settee. When she didn't sit, he eyed her as he squeezed her hand. Iris glanced at her skirt and pulled her hand free, which Tytler released. She lifted her skirt to sit on the settee. He sat beside her and slid closer. When the footman entered, he strode right to her and filled her wine glass to the brim. Her gaze connected with his, and he winked again. Laurel followed with two desserts setting them on the table. Spotted dick. A favorite of Iris's.

Laurel waved to the footman. "Thank ye, Davey." Davey, Iris would have to remember his name. He was a friendly servant. Laurel sat across the room, pretending to mend a shirt she pulled from a basket by the fireplace. Iris knew she kept her eyes trained on them and sighed in relief. At least this time, she wasn't stuck alone with the Lieutenant.

Iris turned to Lieutenant Tytler, who nearly ran his fork of cake into her face. "Please allow me to feed a sweet to my sweet." She took the bite, and he grinned. "Will you do the same, my dear?"

He leaned forward, closed his eyes, and opened his mouth. Iris didn't want to feed this man anything more than horse dung. The image made her giggle, which made Lieutenant Tytler hum. Taking advantage of his closed eyes, Iris spilled wine on them both.

He jerked back as she stood. "Oh, look! How clumsy of me."

Laurel ran to her, grabbing her arm. "Not red wine. Mi'Lady, we must soak that dress now before that stains." As Laurel dragged her from the room, she glanced over her shoulder, shrugging at Lieutenant Tytler.

When they rounded the corner of the first landing of stairs, Laurel whispered, "That was right canny of ye, spilling the wine."

She giggled. "Here, he thought he was getting a bite of a sweet."

Iris snickered with her maid. "Yes, I suspect he would try to kiss me next. I had to do something."

Laurel laughed as they reached the top of the stairs. "All he got was a lap full of wine."

Iris chuckled. "Well, let's hope he got the message. I prefer wine over *his sweet* any day."

Chapter 6

For Iris, the week went by as slow as molasses. She'd ordered three more Gaelic books she had Laurel pick up only to encounter her mother demanding to see the packages, which Laurel did an excellent job of hiding in plain sight, claiming they were on cultural etiquette of a proper English woman.

The day came for her costume fitting, and Iris was ecstatic about her selection for the masked, costumed ball for the New Year. She felt she'd been particularly *canny*, as Laurel put it, and her mother felt her choice was perfect for a cultured *English woman*.

Iris spun again as the tulle and organza fabric glittered in the sunlight from the window. Light blue, like ice, would best describe the color. Mac, the stable master, and Davey had worked together on her wings. Framed in a lightweight tin and covered in the same fabric as her gown, Laurel looped the leather straps on her shoulders as the tiny fairy wings rested on her back.

Laurel grinned as she stepped back. "My, ye look like the queen of the fairies."

Iris smiled. "Because I am. I am Titania from Shakespeare's play *A Midsummer Night's Dream*." Her eyes connected with Laurel's blank stare. "I saw the show in London. I told you about the fairy story. A most spectacular play and for this party fitting."

Laurel turned fingering the mask. "Ahh, the fairy

queen. Let me remember this, right? Titania magically falls in love with a laborer, the weaver, while under a spell. The weaver wears a donkey's head because he feels it's better suited for him."

Her maid handed her the mask, which Iris took and tried on as she spoke, "Yes, and after her husband had enough of watching Titania make a fool of herself to woo *a monster*, he reversed the spell, and the two reunite after Titania announces, 'What visions have I seen! Methought I was enamored of an ass.' " Iris used a high-pitched voice for Titania's line, laughing as she spoke it.

Laurel chuckled. "So, it's the Lieutenant that's the ass?" Iris put the mask on and glanced into the mirror. The facade only covered her eyes, not the whole of her face. And her hair was auburn, a rare color for sure.

She turned to Laurel, her confidante. "The mask only covers part of my face. Alex will recognize me as Ivy in a heartbeat."

Her servant smirked. "Would that be so bad?"

Iris turned back to the mirror. "Yes and no. I'm not ready to tell him. I need the right moment." She hummed. "In the meantime, we need to change my hair. And the mask needs to cover the whole of my face."

Laurel came close and lifted the mask's edge. "We can put fabric on the bottom, trimming it close to yer face, but leave yer mouth open to eat and drink."

Iris fingered her hair as she stared at her reflection in the mirror. "Powder? No, I'd never get this mass all covered. A wig!"

Laurel nodded. "Blonde, maybe even white. We'll see what the merchant has."

Iris's eyes met her friend's in the mirror. "Thank you. I will finally have a chance to meet Alex in person.

Speak with him for once. I would like that."

A knock sounded at her door, and Laurel went to answer it.

Her father stood there, flowers and a letter in hand. "Flowers for Iris from Lieutenant Tytler." Iris stood still, not wanting anything from the *horse beater*. They all stood in awkward stillness for a moment.

Laurel moved and took the flowers from her father. "I'll put these in water." She curtsied.

When she moved past her father, he held up the letter, his eyes on Iris. "Curious this is. A letter from Alex MacDougall." Iris sucked in a breath, and her gaze swung to Laurel.

Her father followed her look. "The curious part isn't him sending a letter. The curious part is that it's for Laurel." He handed the letter to Laurel, and Iris breathed again.

Her father's regard moved between the two women. "Had to pry the paper from the missus' hands. She was about to open the note to see why Alex was interested in a servant. I refused to allow her such an invasion of privacy."

Laurel took the letter and bowed out. "Thank ye, Mi'Lord." Behind her father, she winked as she waved the letter.

Her father strode into the room. "You look like a goddess, Iris."

She smiled at him. "I am. I am Titania." She twirled like when she was a little girl with a new dress finishing gazing into the mirror.

Her father chuckled. "From the Shakespeare play." He came closer and stared at her in the reflection. "Fitting, you as a Fairy Queen."

He waved to a chair as he sat in the opposite one. "I came to speak to you, Iris." Iris took the wings off and set them aside as she turned and sat, wondering what her father wanted to speak of.

He sat forward, taking her hands in his. "About Lieutenant Tytler." Iris sighed, removed her hands, and sat back.

Her father leaned back and eyed her. "It's as I suspected, isn't it? You don't like him, do you?"

Iris rolled her eyes speaking plainly to her father. "He doesn't respect me. He doesn't ask my opinion or permission on anything." His kiss came to her mind, and the beating of the horse brought on a shiver.

Lord Erskine sat up taller. "He hasn't…been forward with you?" Iris blinked back tears. She'd never had a discussion like this with her father. Would he be angry?

Her sire sat forward and took her hands in his. "Iris, you must be honest with me. I'm here to protect my family, my daughter."

A tear fell as she whispered, "He made his mistake out as my fault, but I wasn't to blame." She breathed, and another tear fell as her father squeezed her hands. "When we rode in the College Gardens, he kissed me without permission." Her father growled, and Iris sat up babbling. "He'd asked what books I read, and I told him *Pamela*." She glanced away. "And well, he took my mention of the book as an invitation."

Her father's gaze followed hers. "What did your maid do?"

Iris' eyes came to his. "There was no maid. Mother arranged the outing. We went alone."

He yanked his hands from hers. "Damn woman

preaches propriety, but when it comes to her matchmaking goals, she throws them all out the window!" His eyes intent on her he asked, "Any other outings or incidents I must know of?" She shivered and glanced away as another tear fell.

Her father stood tapping his hand against his leg. "Iris, I must know."

She stared out the window. "The time I first met him. In the stable yard. I didn't know him, and he didn't know me." She glanced at him. "He beat his horse. Not just a slap to put him in his place, beat him till the horse screamed." She leaned forward, her arms mimicking the motions. "I ran to him without thinking. Grabbed the whip, and he turned on me, ready to hit me. If it hadn't been for Mac, our stable master, the man would have beat me." She looked down. "I don't like him at all."

Her father huffed. "Yes, I noted that at the dinner this last week." He rolled his neck as it popped. "While I understand bringing a rough mount in hand, I cannot abide what you describe. Your mother has allowed too many liberties with the man. I fear he thinks his position is secured."

Iris sat forward. "His position as what?"

Her father clicked his tongue. "I have allowed your mother too much leeway. She wants Lieutenant Tytler to offer for your hand and us to accept on your behalf."

Iris stood. "But you promised the choice would be my decision." She paced. This can't be happening! She wanted Alex but needed more time, time for him to meet her as Iris, not Ivy. Why did everything have to be so hard? Why couldn't her mother allow her to find her own friends? Husband or not, she wanted to do things on her own.

She stopped, and her father watched her with a keen eye. "You've met another, haven't you?"

Iris stammered, "I, I mean,"

She twirled and sat hard in her chair. "I don't know what to do!"

Her father took her hands in his with a soft smile on his face. "One step at a time, daughter. First, you don't like Lieutenant Tytler. I will have your mother stop her pursuit. I will also let him know I shall escort you to the ball. You're not spoken for, thus, no one shall attend you but me. That should cool his heels a bit."

Tears gathered in her eyes as she whispered, "Thank you, Father."

He smiled as he held her hands. "Step two, get out more. Meet new friends." When she went to speak, he held his hand up. "I will speak with your mother. Your friends, not hers."

He bent and kissed her cheek. "Step three, dry your tears, daughter. There are many eligible bachelors in Glasgow. Maybe we'll have luncheon next week, eh? I have a bachelor in mind for you to meet. The High Tea Room?"

Iris sucked in a breath as he dropped her hands. Certainly, he hadn't seen her with Alex. When her gaze met his he winked before he turned and strolled to the door.

He stopped and smirked. "Titania at the ball. Will you cast a spell, fall for an ass, or find your love?"

****

Three days later, Iris and Laurel sneaked down the back staircase of the manor house—the one reserved for servants. Each had the Comyn arisaid rolled, tucked, and concealed under their arms. Both women wove their way through the kitchen with their heads down. Iris had covered her head with a long scarf and kept her gaze down. If any servant noted the lord's daughter, no one mentioned anything.

When they reached the back door, her mother's shrill voice echoed. "Where is my tea? And I want those cakes from that Scot's tearoom." Iris stiffened and Laurel shoved her out the door before her mother entered the kitchen, ruining their planning.

They trod to the supply wagon that Mac had hitched a team to. Both women climbed into the back. When Mac strode by, he grinned and winked at them. Was the whole manor house included in her weekly excursions to the Gaels meetings?

She turned to Laurel. "Why'd you have to burn the letter? I wanted to see it for myself."

Laurel sighed. "I told ye before. Yer mother and her crabbit ways prying into everyone's business."

Mac climbed into the driver's seat. "Another detour by the slaughterhouse ladies?" Iris sat silent as did Laurel. He chuckled when there was no response and cued the horses to trot out of the stable yard.

Once away from her family's manor house, Iris sat up. "Tell me all he said again. I want to know."

Mac chuckled. "Got it bad for him, doesn't she?"

Iris grumbled and turned to Laurel, who had to speak loudly over the clomp of the horse's hoofs. "My dearest love of my life," she said in a high-pitched, whiny tone as she fluttered her lashes.

She hit her, and Laurel broke out in a laugh. "He begged ye to come to the meeting. He asked if ye'd stay late. Wants to walk ye home, which ye cannot allow to happen." She huffed. "Yer mother should work for the crown. She's a good spy."

Iris moaned. "I wish I could have seen it, held it. His first letter to me, and because of my meddlesome mother, you had to burn it. I wanted to keep it."

Laurel patted her hand. "I suspect there will be many more letters between ye both."

Iris glanced at her dearest friend. "Didn't you say John sent a letter for you as well?"

Her maid blushed. "Aye, and I won't tell ye what John said. No matter how much ye ask me."

Mac called out. "Bridge Street. This is where I drop ye lovely ladies." He stopped the wagon, and both women climbed out. He glanced between them both. "Aye, ye sure ye don't want me swinging back by to pick ye both up?"

Iris shook her head as she unfolded the Comyn arisaid and wrapped the fabric around her head. "No, Mac, we'll be fine."

He eyed her for a moment. "Gash, miss. With yer auburn hair, ye look like my sister ye do. A fine Scottish lass."

Iris smiled. "Thank you, Mac." Mac clicked to the team, and the wagon rolled away.

Laurel elbowed her. "We are close, please don't speak."

Both women turned to see Alex and John approach on horseback. Iris gaped at them and quickly clamped her mouth shut. Both men rode war horses, large and heavy mounts meant for fighting. She'd never seen one up close. Her father only kept average mounts and worker horses for the wagon, and while large, these were nearly twice their size. Mac outfitted their carriage with two white mares. Her Pixie was a dainty horse meant for short outings and stood at fifteen hands. These easily stood at eighteen or twenty.

Alex's horse pranced, and he called out. "Ho, Oberon!" Iris' eyes went wide at the name. Both men dismounted, and Alex swung his leg over the pommel instead of the back. His plaid flared, giving Iris the most delectable view. *So, the rumor was true—Scots wore nothing under their plaid.* Her face heated moving to the roots of her hairline as she approached Alex.

He patted the horse and handed the reins to a boy. "Hold them well, Timmy."

The youth grinned. "Aye, Laird."

Iris reached out to pet the animal, and Alex grabbed her hand. "Careful. He's a trained warhorse." He held her hand in his. "Ye must be introduced or find yerself bitten." He gathered her in his arms, holding her as they approached the animal.

Alex's deep timbre vibrated along her neck as he spoke. "Oberon, this is the lovely lady, Ivy." His body came flush with hers, and heat spread across her back. When they moved together, his muscles shifted in a most delightful way against her, making her breath hitch. He held her hand as he stretched toward the horse's nose. The animal's breath blew hard against her skin.

She jolted as Alex held her tighter to him. "Do not be afraid. He smells me mixed with ye." He petted the soft nose with her hand, and the horse bowed his head. Alex moved till they scratched the forelock, and Ivy giggled. He stepped back but didn't release her. She pointed to the horse and Alex, then her lips.

Alex laughed. "Ye want to kiss my horse?"

She blew a breath, this mimicking quickly became tiresome. She made the crown over her head, then made her hands into wings at her sides and pointed to the horse.

Alex grinned. "Ah, his name. Oberon, King of the Fairies from Shakespeare's play." He eyed the black stallion. "I felt he was magical and deserved a good name." Oberon stomped and tossed his head as if to agree.

Alex laughed. "It's a name that describes his temperament well."

He nodded to Timmy and led her to the meeting area as he weaved them through the crowd. Many greeted Alex warmly and nodded to her. When he arrived in the middle of the gathering, she made to move away, and he held her to his side.

He took a flask from his sporran and handed the bottle to her. "I promised I'd have a tot for ye the next time I'd see ye." He pulled another and lifted the decanter as he called out to the crowd. "To whisky and to Scotland!"

Everyone replied, "Slainte!" some tipping their drink, others turning back to their chatter. Iris opened hers and took a sip. The same whisky from the luncheon filled her mouth. Heady with a nip.

A man called out from the back. "No speech tonight, Alex?"

Alex shook his head. "No, visit and take yer ease, all of ye." Many mingled, and the volume rose. Alex moved them to the side by the pub. The pub sat quieter tonight than previous meeting nights.

Alex held his arm around her as he leaned against the bridge's support pole. "Have another wee nip, Ivy." He clinked their flasks together and took a long pull on his. She took another sip—the burn a welcome respite. Alex fingered the decorations from the pub window.

They'd added mistletoe since the last meeting.

He plucked the greenery from the wreath and twirled the plant in his fingers. "Mistletoe." Iris picked at the plant, and Alex let her hold it. He pocketed his flask, took hers, closed it, and did the same.

He pulled her till she leaned against him. "My grandmother started a family tradition long before I was born. We cut greenery boughs each Christmas and bring them indoors to symbolize life, rebirth, and renewal. My mother continued the tradition and always spoke about it."

His voice took on an *otherworldly* tone—the brogue deeper, as if he recited the words like his ancestors. "The ancient people believed the Yuletide greenery had power over death because the green never faded. Thus, they used evergreens to defeat winter demons and hold back death and destruction."

His r's rolled more as he spoke about his tradition, enchanting Iris. "My mother said the Yuletide greenery was to encourage the Sun's return because of their strength and tenacity. The Druids held nothing more sacred than the mistletoe and the tree on which the plant grew, a hardy oak. Druids considered mistletoe to be magical because they grow without soil. We add the mistletoe to the evergreen for luck."

He took the sprig from her and twisted the item between his fingers. "She always said a kiss under the mistletoe at Hogmanay from yer love will bring good luck for the year through." He held the leaves over her head. "A kiss, Ivy, can I kiss ye?" Iris's eyes went wide, moved to his lips, then returned to his eyes. She wanted this so badly—a kiss from Alex.

She nodded as he grinned. He held the mistletoe

over her head and softly brushed his lips against hers. When she returned the kiss, his arms encircled her, the mistletoe forgotten. She gasped, and his tongue slid into her mouth, dancing with hers. Her body flashed hot, then cold. He growled into the kiss and turned her till he backed her against the pole as he shifted them deeper into the shadows.

She'd never had a kiss like this that burned and chilled at once—the warmth of his lips and his tongue's movement in a sensual rhythm. Lieutenant Tytler's kiss was wet bread compared to this. Alex shifted them again as he kissed his way down her neck. Her knees nearly buckled when he returned to her ear, suckling the lobe.

Alex's breath tickled her as he whispered, "God, Ivy, I've wanted to kiss ye like that since the first day I saw ye." His lips returned to hers, and she kissed him with all her heart. Her tongue matched his movements. Soon, his hands roamed her body and heat flashed over her again. He pressed against her, and his arousal brushed her stomach, sending tingles over her body. The hot, and cold, all she wanted was this man to hold, kiss, and love her. He growled as he kissed her neck again. Pure desire shot through her, and she moaned deeply in her throat. For the next while, Iris felt as if the world had been handed to her. Alex's kisses stoked a flame of passion and a bit more. Could she be entertaining the idea of love? Would it be possible after only knowing him for a bit? When Alex moved back to her lips and moved deeper into the heat of their desire, Iris could only hold on to the realization that this Scot, this man, was indeed a man she could love.

Laurel called out, "Ivy." Her heart hammered in her ears. The call came louder this time, sterner, "Ivy, Ivy!"

Alex stopped and rested his head on her shoulder as he tried to catch his breath. "Laurel calls. Ye must go."

Iris felt she'd run the whole way from her manor house. She was so out of breath. How had he done this to her with mere kisses? He held her tightly as he sidestepped out of the shadows and held her at arm's length when they came into the light from the pub.

Laurel stood aside. "Ivy, 'tis late. We *must* go now!"

Alex kissed her cheek. "Ye go. We'll see each other again next week. I promise." He pushed the mistletoe into her hand. "Save this for a kiss from me under the mistletoe at Hogmanay."

He kissed her again. "Till next week." He ambled away, followed by John. Alex tossed a coin to Timmy and mounted Oberon. He turned the animal around once and nodded to her, then kneed his horse into a gallop and took off into the night.

Chapter 7

The following week, Iris and Laurel approached the Gaels meeting. Timmy was at his post holding the horses as men's voices raised in anger echoed from under the bridge. "Ye ladies better hang out here. The English got them all up in a dander."

Iris exchanged a glance with Laurel, who whispered to the youth, "What is it that's got them upset?"

Timmy leaned against the pole. "I heard Alex tell them Daniel and Rees Williamson along with Gamaliel Davies, the printers, beat Jacob Thomas, one of the British officers of Glasgow in an attempt to get Ness McNabb out of the red coat's, as Alex put it, *unlawful custody*. The officer said McNabb wore a plaid and spoke in Gaelic. That made the gobber mad so the red coat got more of his friends and arrested all four. Called them Jacobites. They are set to hang." He spit on the ground. "Not even Officer Drake is around tonight."

Iris gaped as Laurel patted her hand. "I'm sure it will be all right."

Both women ducked into the meeting area as men raised their fists and one shouted, "It's their way of taking us down again!"

Another yelled, "The focking English want to kill us all!"

One on Iris's right bellowed, "Kill the English— let's take Scotland back!"

78

The men shifted and swarmed the center, where Alex stood over the crowd as if on his raised box. Iris was too short and far back to see much more.

He raised his arms. "Now, quiet down, everyone. We can't all run off killing people. There is a reasonable way to free the men. Let me work on it, and I'll let ye know." He turned, eyeing the men. "Courts take time."

A man bellowed out, "Alex, ye know damn well the courts are a ploy, something to placate us. That bloody Lieutenant Tytler went to the sheriff and demanded the men to hang. No trial at all!"

Iris gasped, and the men before her glanced her way, then back at the crowd. Wasn't her father over the courts? Couldn't he do something for those men? Lieutenant Tytler wouldn't demand people be killed unless there was a crime, would he?

Alex roared over the crowd. "Calm down." He turned again and shouted louder, *"Calma síos!"* Men shoved her from behind, and she fell forward on her hands and knees.

Laurel cried out, "Ivy!" She grabbed her, but someone tugged her arms away.

Timmy hollered from behind them. "Redcoats! They come on horseback with torches."

Alex bellowed, "Away, everyone away!"

Laurel screamed from far away. "Ivy!"

Many in the crowd shouted. People pushed and trampled Iris as she curled into a ball. A kick to the stomach had her crying out. Another stepped on her head. There was so much yelling and screaming that the sounds all echoed into a pounding in her head.

Someone stomped on her chest, and her breath left her. She pulled in air, trying to breathe, but she couldn't.

Her head spun, and the world tilted. This was it—this would be how she would die.

Strong arms grabbed her and picked her up as she gulped in a large breath of air. She grabbed the nearest item—a red plaid as someone cradled her against a warm, hard chest. She heaved another breath as she found herself carried by someone who ran.

Alex yelled in her ear as his chest vibrated with force. "Timmy, run, go!" He jostled her again. "John, split up! Circle around, stay to the alleys." They moved upward together, then again, as a horse shifted under them. Iris buried her face into the chest, knowing Alex held her.

John shouted. "Aye, I have Laurel."

They took off on the horse at a run as Alex whispered, "*luas dhiathan*" *God's speed.* They galloped for some time, but the patterned clatter of Oberon's hoofs almost soothed her.

He drew up, stopping the horse as she nearly fell off. "Damn it all." His grip on her tightened as she held his plaid harder.

An English accent clipped as a British soldier called out. "They scatter like fleas. Search every alley." Lieutenant Tytler, no, it can't be him!

Alex swung the horse away and walked him farther down the lane. He guided the horse into the darkened alley and slid off, holding her. He sat her down on a crate. When he pulled up, she still held his plaid.

His eyes connected with her as he gripped her hand. "Ivy, ye must let go for a moment. I need to hide my plaid." She stared into his face, half in shadow. His stern expression shifted a bit. When she released him, he stepped around to the other side of Oberon. He stripped his plaid and pulled trews from his saddle bag. She glanced away, and her hand went to her head.

Alex's voice startled her. "Ye lost yer arisaid. Don't worry, lass. I have a plan."

When she glanced back, he'd come back around the horse. Alex had covered his legs and tucked his plaid into his saddle bag. As he pulled out his flask he dumped the contents on the front of his shirt. He topped the flask and shoved the bottle back into the bag.

Alex knelt before her, brushing his hand along her cheek. "Ivy, lass. Ye must play along. We are to be drunkards, aye?" He pulled her to stand, and her legs gave out. He swept her in his arms. "Not much longer, lass, I have ye."

He held her tight as he climbed atop Oberon. He shifted her, and the scent of whisky flooded her nose. As his arm connected with her bruised ribcage, she jolted.

His breath tickled her ear. "Play passed out, lass." He kneed his horse, who grunted with the extra weight. She gripped him as they emerged before two English officers.

Alex swung in the saddle as he yelled in a surprisingly good English accent slurred with the drink. "Long live the King!"

With his next swerve, she nearly fell from the seat, and he pulled her closer. "I've got me a trollop tonight!"

One of the officers called, "Move on, drunkard. We seek the rebel Scots."

Alex pushed his horse to a trot as he called over his shoulder. "Happy hunting!"

He moved along at a controlled pace as he held her. "Stay with me, Ivy. We are almost home."

They met no one else on the road. Ivy must have

dozed off because when Alex dismounted from his horse, she woke with a start.

His arms squeezed her once. "Almost inside, then we'll see to yer injuries." He elbowed into the house and took the stairs, carrying her easily.

They moved down a hallway, and John stepped out of a room. "Laurel is with me safe. How's Ivy?" Alex kept walking until he came to a door at the end of the hallway. John opened it, and Alex moved her to the chair before the roaring fire.

John chuckled. "Did ye stop by the bar on the way home? Ye smell like it."

Alex pulled away. "Played drunkards to get away."

John stood at the door. "I had Bertha set some water in a pot over yer fire. Cloth for bandages and necessities are next to it."

Iris went to stand, and Alex placed his hand on her shoulder. "Ye stay put till I see to yer injuries." She shook her head, and a wave of dizziness hit her hard. She lay back and moaned.

John spoke from the door. "Ivy, Laurel says ye're to get home early so as not to make the missus angry." She was too tired and in pain to care, so she didn't reply.

The door clicked close, and Iris closed her eyes, willing the pain to recede as Alex shuffled about. The clink of tin and the creak of something metal came to her. He moved about again. When a cold cloth came to her head, she jumped. Her gaze went to Alex's as tears flooded her eyes.

He bent over her. "Shh, lassie. 'Tis only a bump on the head." She shifted and cringed to her side.

His eyes moved to her ribs, then her face. "I'll be right back, Ivy." Alex bent and kissed her forehead.

More scuffling, then silence. The sound of liquid pouring filled the air. More scraping, then silence again. He returned and knelt before her with two glasses full of whisky and a plaid over his arm. He'd changed shirts, and his hair fell loose to his shoulders.

Alex set the glasses on the side table and bent to pick her up. Her hand held the cloth to her head as he turned. When he lifted her in his arms, their faces came even. She gazed into his eyes, and they creased in concern. He sat and rested her in his lap. When he brushed her rib cage, she sucked in a breath. He pulled the plaid from the chair and wrapped them inside, making a warm cocoon. He handed her a glass, and she took it.

He took his own. "Sip, Ivy. I think ye have more than the head injury." She took a sip and moaned as she leaned into his warmth. He took a healthy swig and set the glass aside.

His hands moved along her back, testing each area. "Where? In yer ribs?" When he hit her lower right side, she sucked in a breath. He sat her forward and pulled on her laces as the cloth on her head fell into her lap. She reached for his hand and winced again.

His hand stopped. "At ease. I only loosen them to slide a heated cloth there."

She nodded and sipped her drink, welcoming the burn down her throat.

He grunted. "I suspect the pressure from yer corset is not helping the pain." When the stays loosened, she took a deep breath relieved to be free of the constraints. He bent and selected a cloth from the kettle beside the chair. The fabric steamed. When he slid the material between her shift and skin, she jolted. He tsked as he maneuvered the heated pad into place. As he removed his hand and pulled her back into his embrace, she exhaled feeling the heat soothe her aches. Alex picked up the cooled cloth, placed the pad on her head, and embraced her.

They lounged in the chair momentarily; the heat easing her ache, the whisky numbing the pain. As the evening's events came back to her, she gulped the rest of her drink.

Alex chuckled and took the glass from her. "Ah, the shock and daze of the evening wearing off now?"

She glanced up as his eyes wandered her face. His fingers probed the bruise at the back of her head making her wince and shift back. She pulled her hands out of the covers as Alex watched each movement. Her hands made the crown sign as he smiled, then pointed at him. She made her fingers like a galloping horse. He moved to grab her hands, and she pulled back. But when she made the horse run away again, he glanced away. Iris poked his chest, and he glanced at her as she shook her head.

Alex brushed his hand on her cheek. "Ye are a canny lass. I suppose I understand all ye ask. Aye, I'll share my thoughts with ye, even if they do or don't answer yer questions."

He held her as he rested his head back in the chair. "Ye are concerned about the English officers?" She nodded, and he didn't look down, likely feeling her movement.

Squinting at the ceiling, he spoke, "I didn't appoint myself the Gaels leader. No one asked. It just happened. I suppose my position at the courts led to that. Helping to bridge the gap between the English and Scots." He glanced down. She reached her hand to his cheek, repeating his sentiment, hoping he would read her feelings.

Alex hummed. "I admit, I like the role—leading. I suppose it's natural. I am to be Laird one day."

He breathed and rested his head back again. "The English. That's a bother. They'd not been overly active till late. For the most part, they'd allowed our *cultural meetings* as long as we abide by the crown's rule." Lieutenant Tytler's presence hit her memory. She sat forward and gave a salute. The movement caused her to gasp.

Alex held her. "Ivy, do not move so fast. Ye are still bruised." She lay back and sighed. She pointed at him, saluted, and then to him again. Iris wanted him to understand Lieutenant Tytler deeply hated all Scots. Alex needed a warning.

He shook his head. "Enough talk about the English. That is the last thing I wish to do with you."

As Alex's hand shifted to her cheek, then her chin, he tilted her and brushed his lips against hers. He skimmed them again, and she opened to his kisses as heat spread over her body. Alex's tongue slid in, and he lightly pulled her to him as he deepened the kiss. She moved with him, her injuries easily forgotten. All she wanted was Alex and his kisses.

His lips broke away, trailing them to her ear as he breathed. "Ivy, I've wanted to kiss ye endlessly since I met ye." As he nipped her ear he whispered, "Let me give ye a taste of my love. I promise we do what ye'll like." He lifted his head as he stared at her, waiting for her permission. She nodded, fully trusting Alex. He'd never do anything she didn't want. All she had to do was signal to stop. Alex bent into her and kissed her harder, shifting her to straddle his lap. She felt sexy and a little wanton, like *Pamela*, but with her love. While he kissed her neck, he pulled her hairpins loose. Their ping on the wood flooring sounded above the rustle of clothing. Her hair fell free, and she shook her tresses loose. He pulled on her bodice till her breasts fell free.

Alex moaned, "Beautiful." Then, cupped them both, bent and laved a nipple. Bolts of desire shot through her as her hand roamed his chest. He pulled a hand free, took her wrist in his, and lowered her palm to the top of his pants. Her gaze followed, and he raised an eyebrow to ask permission. She wanted to explore so much of him, of them. She bent and kissed him hard. Alex's response was to chuckle into the kiss. He undid the buttons and slid her hand, guiding her to wrap her fingers around his hard shaft. He kissed her hard as he guided her hand up and down over him. When he took his hand away as he bent to kiss her breast, she kept her hand there, repeating the movements.

Alex sucked in a breath. "Ye're a quick study."

She stroked him again, and he threw his head back in a groan. Iris marveled at the control she had over him. She stroked him again, and his hands squeezed her breasts. Tingly heat flashed over her body. She moved down on him again. His entire body jolted as he growled.

Alex sat up and flipped her skirts up as he kissed her hard. "I must return the favor." Iris jumped at the contact of his hand on her thigh. His eyes drifted open.

She held him as he flitted his fingers over her flesh, sending sparks over her body. "Is this what ye want, Ivy? To feel a man, bring ye to pleasure without taking from ye?"

Her response was to stroke him harder and faster.

He growled as his finger moved over her folds. Once, she'd touched herself that way after Laurel explained the act and had a moment of pleasure, but this was something entirely different. The intimacy of each one touching the other to bring mutual pleasure. This was what she wanted, what she'd read about, what she craved.

Moisture flooded her folds as she felt something build inside of her. She kept her pace on him as he shifted a finger into her, and pressure, like nothing she'd experienced, built in her. He moved in and out. Picking up on his rhythm, she mimicked his pace. They kissed and moved with each other in a dance of pleasure. Heat flashed, the pressure built, and she yelped. The dam exploded as light burst behind her eyelids. Alex held her there as he cried out as well. Wetness flooded her hand, and she withdrew as he panted. The pressure faded, and she fell on him limp and spent resting her forehead on his shoulder. He shifted her to the side and pulled the now-cooled cloth from her ribs. As he slid from the chair, he knelt before her. Alex wiped her, then himself. When he stood, he buckled his pants, leaving the top undone.

Tossing the cloth aside, he lifted her, settled her lying in his lap again, and she curled into his embrace. His heartbeat lulled her to a dreamlike state.

He brushed her hair away from her face. "Sleep, Ivy. Heal and rest. Tomorrow will come too soon." She sighed and drifted off.

****

Iris woke to a tapping on her arm. Her eyes connected with Laurel's in the low firelight as her maid placed her finger to her lips. Alex's arms had relaxed in his sleep and no longer embraced her. She easily slid from his lap.

He shifted and muttered. "Ivy."

Iris froze half out of his embrace. She and Laurel stilled a moment till his light snores came again. She rose and stood as she studied him in his slumber. He had a boyish look about him, his hair tousled as low snores rumbled from his nose. She could wake to this every day.

Laurel pinched her. When Iris whipped around, Laurel nodded to the doorway. Iris took a step, and her foot hit her hairpins. She bent and picked up as many as she could find. When she rose, Laurel's eyes went wide and waved her out of the room. At the doorway, she glanced back at Alex, asleep in his chair. God, how she wanted this, them.

Laurel led them down the darkened stairs, through the blessedly vacant kitchens, and into the stable yard. Iris tried to fix her stays, and Laurel whipped her around, tightening them quickly, forcing a gasp from her at the pinch to her ribs. As Laurel stepped away, Iris ran her hands through her hair, piled the mass atop her head, and pinned the strands in place with as many pins as possible. Laurel returned with two plaid wraps. When Iris made to speak, her maid put her hand over her mouth and shook her head.

In the dark, they made their way on foot back home. Iris followed Laurel, who seemed to know every alley and cranny, allowing them to go unnoticed on foot from Alex's home to hers

Neither spoke.

When they neared her home over an hour later, Iris finally broke the silence. "You know your way well."

Laurel glanced back. "Aye, and don't tell anyone."

She turned, but Iris grabbed her hand. "What of

tonight?"

Laurel smiled. "Did ye like it? Yer time with Alex?"

Iris's face heated. "Yes, and he was very respectable."

Laurel turned, and Iris stopped her again. "Can we go again tonight?"

She rolled her eyes. "Lord, what have I started? I'll be fired for sure."

****

Alex woke with a start, his arms empty.

He sat up and twisted around. "Ivy?" He stood, nearly ran to the door, and opened it as John stood there, ready to knock. Alex came up short.

John sighed. "They are gone." Alex rubbed his hand over his face as he turned back into the room.

His friend shifted inside after him. "Early, before dawn. George spied them leaving through the stable yard as he came to begin his day." Alex picked up his whisky glass, filled it, and downed it.

With a quick sweep of the room, John took in the unruly chair, an abandoned plaid, and various items beside it. "Ye slept in the chair?" His gaze fell on the made-up bed. "Not the bed?"

Alex slammed the glass on the table. "She may be a maid, but she still has her virtue."

John bent picking up a hairpin from the floor and held the clip between them. "Her hairpin, silver. A high-quality item for a maid, don't ye think?" He handed the pin to Alex, who examined the thick, glittering metal. He set her item on the table, gathered his plaid, and folded the fabric.

As he set his tartan on the bed, John set a log on the fire. "Strange, when I first saw them that day in the street.

I could have sworn Laurel was the maid and Ivy the Lady. Laurel was behind her carrying boxes." Alex put the kettle over the ashes from the fire. The embers long burned out, now catching flame again with the addition of wood.

John picked up the bandages and handed them to Alex. "A riddle, for sure."

Alex threw the fabric on the chair. "The riddle we need to solve is why the English are suddenly so interested in our activities after allowing us to carry on so long." He paced. "What's changed? And why did they treat Daniel and Rees Williamson, and Gamaliel Davies barbarically? Ness McNabb as well." He ran his hands through his hair. "What's egged them on?"

John shrugged. "I'll ask around and see what we can find out." He sighed. "See if Lord Erskine can get ye a meeting with them, get them off the hanging." Alex nodded in agreement.

Alex's gaze rose fast. "Ivy was injured. Can we arrange a visit to her?"

John shook his head. "Laurel said the missus of the house is strict. Ye must send a note to Laurel."

A note. What would Alex say to the woman he might have found love with again?

Chapter 8

Bam! *Bam*! *Bam*! Lord Erskine pounded his gavel amidst the yelling and hollering in the courtroom. "Order, I will have order, or I'll place each of you in jail!"

Alex stood in the center of chaos, wondering how everything had come to this. The English pitted against the Scottish again over a long portion of fabric and a centuries-old language. Today, no one even argued who the King was. Lord Erskine eyed him from his place above all on his raised desk. Alex groaned. This would prove to be a difficult day.

An English officer moved through the crowd. "You heard the Lord. Quiet down, all of you!"

The room's rumble lowered as people retook their seats. Alex looked at his fellow Scotsmen, charged with hanging for practicing their culture.

Daniel and Rees Williamson, and Gamaliel Davies were printers, not warriors. Certainly, they did not need to make them an example of English rule over Scotland. Ness McNabb, their printing partner, sat beside them. Despite sporting a black eye and busted lips, he smiled back at Alex. They all counted on him. Hell, Lord Erskine depended on him.

Their conversation from a few days before filled his mind.

James Erskine paced his chambers. "Alex, I don't

understand it. Everything's gone so well over the last two years. The last killing of a Jacobite was so long ago and not even under my rule. From what I understand, he deserved it." James exhaled. "But this, it's outright murder." He paced again. "The rumblings within the English ranks of officers stationed here have risen against the Scots, and I must find out who is behind it all. We must have order and create a sense of unity." His superior and longtime friend strode to him, placing his hand on Alex's shoulder. "I need you to free them, Alex. Lawfully. Convince the people of Glasgow that they are truly innocent." He patted his shoulder, and the task's weight felt much heavier than his simple hand.

The murmurs in the court had died down, bringing Alex to the present. Now, up to him, he turned from the crowd back to Lord Erskine. His gaze caught Lieutenant Tytler's, who gave him the evil eye—a look his grandmother often spoke of—a glare filled with hate, malice, and pure evil. She claimed the person who gave one must have an evil Fae that rested within warning to be wary of him. A chill pressed down his spine, and the reminder of his duty came forth in his mind. Of all the times to think of the magic Iona Stones and Balor, the King of the Evil Fae, now was not it. Still, a wave of evil washed over him, haunting him.

The crown representative that prosecuted the guilty had already delivered their closing arguments. Many an English officer had testified that they'd heard and seen Ness McNabb meeting and speaking out against the crown. Alex was a member of the Gaels and met with the group often. The only place they discussed things so openly was the Gaels meetings. For Ness to truly be guilty of all placed before him, the blame might fall at the entire group's feet.

He faced the crowd instead of Lord Erskine and began his closing arguments. "Ness McNabb, a family man and printer. A humble man not given to excessive drink or fight. He wasn't at the battle of Culloden, yet the man is charged with being a Jacobite." Alex scoffed. "Why, Ness is no more Jacobite than I, you, or you." He turned pointing to various members of the audience. Irony at that, while this wasn't a trial by jury, the people in the courtroom certainly watched the performance and made the judgment, even if the final ruling wasn't theirs to make.

He pointed to the accused and his friends beside him. "Daniel Williamson, Rees Williamson, Gamaliel Davies, and Ness McNabb own a printing press. The *Aberdeen's Journal*. A progressive, liberal paper pushing the unity of Scotland and England." He turned to the audience, wiggling his fingers. "As well as all the delectable tidbits of town gossip." The room broke into laughter.

He spread his arms wide. "Why, even when the great fire of seventeen hundred fifty-one took half the city, the *Aberdeen's Journal* printed dedications *for free*. Free for those who'd lost friends, family, and compatriots. Regardless of English or British heritage, the city of Glasgow came together, and these men were all a part of it." He leaned his hip against his desk, facing the audience and not Lord Erskine, for that was who he truly needed to convince of these men's innocence.

He broke into his Scots accent. "Aye, a Scotsman they may be, but aren't all those here who were born and bred in Scotland—Scots?" He pointed to the people in attendance. "Aren't ye all Scots? Is it a crime to be born

Scottish?"

Murmurs spread through the courtroom, many a Scot nodding as some English tilted their heads in question. Alex turned and caught Lieutenant Tytler's expression, filled with hatred and malice. Let him be angry. This was Scotland, and Alex would rot in hell before he'd allow a fellow Scotsman, who openly followed the crown, to fall for any hate crime of some zealous English officer.

He faced Lord Erskine. "They are law-abiding businessmen, reporting on the politics of Glasgow. They write about the culture of Scotland and the racy tidbits that keep us all buying their newspaper." He nodded. "Aye, the report on the atmosphere of Glasgow is English and Scots alike, but they are true to the crown. They deserve to retain their innocence." Alex nodded again, turned, and walked to his seat. When he sat, he caught Lord Erskine's eye, who nodded.

Lord Erskine shuffled his papers, pulled one out, and cleared his throat. "I am ready to give my judgment." All rose in the courtroom. Alex's heart skipped. Had he done a good enough job on character? Had he shown they were law-abiding citizens? God, he hoped so. The time for hanging Scots was over. The time to start a new Scotland was at hand.

The Justice lifted the paper and read. "For the charge of Jacobite traitor of Ness McNabb, The verdict. Not proven." Lieutenant Tytler stood so fast his chair toppled. Lord Erskine raised his eyebrow at the man. The Lieutenant needed to learn his place. A lower officer was never above a Lord or High Counselor of the Scottish court.

Lord Erskine sighed. "The charges of assault of

Jacob Thomas, officer to the English army from Daniel Williamson, Rees Williamson, and Gamaliel Davies I must find guilty." The court erupted in yells and scuffles.

The Justice banged his gavel. "Order!"

He took a deep breath, seemingly calm, and spoke evenly. "The assault charge is a minor crime, usually handled in the sheriff's court. But I must rule since the initial charge was traitor to the crown." Lord Erskine's eye roamed the room. All sat in stillness, awaiting his verdict.

"The three men shall serve labor clearing the land for the new courthouse. Five hundred manual labor hours per person." He swung his gavel as the court reporter marked the ruling in his journal. Alex turned to his fellow Scots as each hugged the other.

Ness took him in a huge hug. "Alex, ye are the spirit and heart of Scotland." Alex nodded. The court members filed out. He sat, stacked his papers, and placed them in his carry case.

When he stood to leave, Lieutenant Tytler stood before him. They eyed each other for a moment.

The Lieutenant leaned toward him, whispering, "You filthy Jacobites will get what's coming to you. All of you. You dirty up the fine culture of the King's land, and I shall see you all hang."

Alex grinned at him. "The law shall always prevail, Lieutenant. The truth will always win."

As Alex turned to leave, Lieutenant Tytler grabbed his arm. "You are all Jacobites, every last Scot, and I'm coming for you next."

Alex smiled and hissed back, *"Tha mi a faicinn an uilc am broinn thu. Bi deiseil, tha mi deiseil dhut." I see the evil inside you. Be ready, I'm ready for you.* Alex yanked his arm from the Lieutenant and strode from the courtroom.

****

Iris stood beside Laurel in front of the High Tea Room, waiting for her father and two of his chosen eligible bachelors for her to meet. She'd agreed to luncheon instead of another afternoon of tea with her mother's friends. As she tried to contain her nerves, she shifted from foot to foot. Iris patted her hair again, secured in a net with a black straw wide-brimmed hat Laurel insisted she wear. The dark weave holding her hair in place made her chignon almost black instead of her vibrant auburn.

Laurel smirked at her. "Ye look right fine. I promise ye. Ye will enjoy today's meal and company."

Iris shook her head, the pins pulling and the weight of the hat tilting her head. "I don't know, Laurel. I look forward to meeting anyone my father suggests, but I'd rather see Alex."

As if on cue, her father appeared in the crowd beside her. "Another crush again. Seems High Tea Room is the place to be." He peered back into the group. "My colleague will be along soon with his man." Her father turned to her and smiled. "Iris, you look stunning." He bent and kissed her cheek. Her forehead, not an option, since her tilted hat nearly covered one eye.

An all too familiar voice spoke from behind her. "Lord Erskine, this must be yer lovely daughter Iris." Iris stiffened but didn't turn.

Her gaze met Laurel's, who smirked as John took her hand and kissed the back. "Laurel, so good to see you again."

Alex's voice rumbled behind her. "Laurel, I hope

yer cousin is doing well. Please let her know I think of her." *He's thinking of me, worried for me?*

Laurel mumbled a response as she winked at Iris. "Aye, I will."

Her father hummed. "Mr. MacArthur, I wasn't aware you and Laurel were already acquainted. How lovely." He pulled on her arm. "Iris, come now, meet my best solicitor and dearest friend, Lord Justice Clerk to Scotland. Alex MacDougall." *Oh, God, this was it. My game of playing Ivy is at an end. Maybe he wouldn't recognize me if I kept my face hidden for most of the meal.* As Iris turned, she kept her head down, hoping the hat hid her face well enough.

Alex took her hand in his, bent over it, but didn't kiss it. A formal, proper greeting. "Mi'Lady. Charmed to meet ye." He held her hand for a moment, and she peeked at him. He grinned.

A man clapped him on the shoulder, breaking the contact. "Great win for ye, Alex. Ye got the printers free from hanging." Iris swiftly lifted her head—*the accused Jacobites who were charged and might hang. Alex got them free?*

Alex nodded at the man as he still held her hand. "Well, Ness is free. The charges of assault carried a punishment." His focus moved to her father's. "But no hanging, not now or in the future."

Her father nodded. "Right you are, Alex. The parliament is due to sign the law this week. No treasonous Jacobite hangings without significant proof. Let's celebrate, shall we?"

Alex's gaze swung to hers and connected. Her eyes went wide, and her heart raced. *Would he recognize her on the spot, give her away?* He tilted his head to the side and squinted a little.

A server approached. "Lord Erskine, your party's table is this way."

Iris pulled her hand from his and spoke in her clipped English. "If you please, release my hand." She had to play up the prim English lady to maintain her disguise. She wasn't ready to reveal her secret.

Alex shook himself. "Sorry, Mi'Lady, for a minute there, I thought you were someone else."

She proceeded him into the establishment. "Must be the lighting."

Iris's knees quaked as Laurel walked beside her, smirking. "This should be fun."

Iris wanted to kick her as she hissed, "You knew, didn't you? That Alex would be here."

As Iris gave her a side-eye, Laurel giggled as she whispered, "Ye could tell him right here and now. Have the pretending end?" A server brought them to a table in the front window, in full view of any passerby. *Great, this just gets better and better every moment.*

Her father waved them to each seat. "John, you and Laurel take up that side. I'll sit here, and Alex, you and Iris take up the left side together." Well, next to the window is good. Maybe she could hide behind the curtains. Alex pulled out a chair as she stared out the window, watching people stride by. He cleared his throat, and Iris jumped.

Alex waved again, and she sat. "Thank you kindly." Alex sat beside her, and their knees brushed, making Iris jolt.

Alex spoke lowly. "My pleasure, Iris." The way he rolled the r in her name, combined with the first time she'd heard her formal name on his lips, had her belly flutter like bird's wings. She took a deep breath. There had to be a way to get through this meal without her worlds colliding. She prayed to God, *please let this go well*. The server placed menus before each person.

Her father peeked at her over her menu as she held hers high between her and Alex. "Iris, why don't you get the seafood dish? It has crabs and salmon, your favorite." He waved. "Alex, you shall order for her. I'll have meat pie. Alex, you?"

Alex set down his menu. "Meat pie it is." He turned to Iris. "So, ye like our fresh fare. Some from London don't."

Iris set her menu down but tilted her head so her hat covered most of her face. "Yes, seafood is my favorite."

Laurel laughed. "Among whisky." She sat up. "I'll have the seafood as well. Ye, John?"

He smirked. "The pie, as always. It's better than my ma's, but don't tell her I said so!" Laurel and John both laughed and bent their heads, muttering to each other.

Her father eyed them and smiled as he turned to Alex. "A celebratory toast. They stock your family label here, right?"

Alex nodded. "Aye, Mabina stocks it."

Her father waved at the waitress. "A round of the Heart of Scotland, and we'll order now." With the orders in and menus away, Iris had nothing more to hide behind.

Alex grinned at her. "Iris, what are yer pursuits while here in Glasgow?"

She turned a little away from him as her father answered. "Actually, Iris doesn't know I know. But you'd be enlightened to know she is fascinated with the Gaelic language."

Iris jerked her head up. "Father!"

As she lifted an eyebrow, her focus went to Laurel, who shrugged her shoulders. "I didn't spill the beans."

Her father laughed. "The book merchant sends me the bills, daughter. It's good you pursue this. The Scottish culture is rich and interesting. It's why I thought maybe meeting the liaison between the English and the Scots would give you a lot to speak about."

Her gaze moved to Alex, who sat covering his smile with his hand. His eyes traveled to hers and stopped. *Oh, no, this was it. She'd be found out now and punished for her secret life.* Alex's eyes moved over her face, then over her hair.

He shook himself and spoke in a smooth cadence. "*Mas i a' Ghàidhlig a tha sibh ag iarraidh nighinn, feumaidh sibh a bruidhinn gu tric.*" *If it's the Gaelic ye want lass, ye must speak it often.* She bent her head, slowing the words down in her mind.

She glanced up. "Speak often?" Alex grinned at her, and her heart sped up. The server arrived with the drinks, setting one before each person.

Her father leaned over and whispered loudly, "Your mother isn't here. Drink up, daughter." His banter made her smile.

Lord Erskine lifted his glass. "To Alex and our successful win!" The others raised their glasses, speaking together, "Sláinte!" Her father glanced between them, then repeated the toast, "Sláinte!"

Lieutenant Tytler appeared at Iris's side. "I never thought I'd see the day a Lord Advocate of Scotland give a toast in an outlawed language."

Her father took a sip from his glass. "Lieutenant, nothing wrong with having a toast between friends." He breathed deeply, obviously enjoying the taste of the liquor.

The Lieutenant turned to Iris, grabbed her free hand, pulled it up, and kissed the back. "Iris, so good to see you, my sweet."

She yanked her hand from his. "Yes, quite." Alex stiffened beside her.

Her sire swirled the whisky glass in the sunlight from the window. "I'd invite you to join us, Lieutenant, but there's no room. And there is the fact we are celebrating *our* win."

The officer's face went red. "No worries, my lord, I wouldn't dine with dirty Scots anyway."

The offending man bent close to Iris's ear. "If you'd like, I can take you away from this, this criminal company." She shied away from him. His invitation was unwelcome.

Alex stood placing himself between Iris and Lieutenant Tytler. "I am certain the lady is comfortable in *her father's* company, Lieutenant."

Her father took another sip of his spirits. "Quite right, Alex."

Lord Erskine leveled his glare upon the lieutenant. "We've spoken of your pursuit of my daughter. Maybe a sterner reminder needs to be in order." The expression her father directed at Lieutenant Tytler she'd seen before. The visage displayed his controlled anger and his command of respect. She glanced at the officer. Her father had looked at him this way before. The man can't be that naive.

Lieutenant Tytler bowed. "At your service, my lord." He glanced at Iris. "Until the ball, Iris."

As he stepped away, she called out. "Oh Lieutenant, please no longer use my familiar. I am Miss Erskine to you." The officer barely glanced over his shoulder but nodded and strode out of the establishment.

As Alex sat, Iris let loose the breath she'd held the entire time Lieutenant Tytler was present. Her father upended his drink, held the liquor in his mouth, and swallowed slowly. Iris did the same, as she and her father shared a smile across the table.

Alex chuckled beside her. "Ye are the second lass I've met that knows how to drink it right."

The server arrived with their dishes. "Here we are." He set each dish before them.

He started to set the fish before Alex, who stopped him and nodded at Iris. " 'Tis for the lady." As they began their meal, Iris struggled with her shell cracker, the crab casing too tough to break.

Her father reached across. "Allow me, daughter."

Alex beat him to it, taking the cracker from her hand their fingers brushing. "I've got it, Mi'Lord." Iris sat in numbed silence as Alex broke her crab shells, repeating the same motions he had when they had dined weeks ago when she ate with him as Ivy. As before, he placed all the best pieces on her plate, wiped his hands, and smiled at her. She stared in mute fascination. He didn't know, he hadn't realized. When he finished his task, she gave him a wobbled grin and slowly ate her meal.

Alex and her father spoke lively about the progress of the new courthouse for the planned square at the end of town. John and Laurel spoke lowly between them, often exchanging bites off each other's plate. It was clear they had fallen hard for each other.

Iris ate in comfortable silence. She watched Alex and his animated conversation with her father, who was very engaged with the man. Obviously, they got along, and the English and Scottish counterparts worked well when debating which area of the building's design represented Scotland and which honored the crown. She'd not seen her father so happy, so carefree. And Alex was so relaxed and engaged while discussing the future development of something he loved so much. Scotland.

The server came beside her breaking her focus. "Take yer plate, Mi'Lady?" Iris numbly nodded.

Her father huffed. "Iris, I've never seen you so quiet before."

Laurel smirked. "Must be the company." Iris shot her maid a hard glare.

Alex sat back. "She reminds me of someone, but I have no idea who. I can't place my finger on it."

Iris replied in a clipped, tight English accent. "I doubt we've met before. A Scot and an English lady." She tapped her napkin to her lips in a very British fashion, like her mother demanded when she was younger. She had to get him off the thought of her as Ivy. She wasn't ready to expose her truth, and certainly not in front of her father.

Her father signed the check. "Alex, it's back to the office for me. You, my dear chap, may take the afternoon off." He rose. "I'll leave you two to bid the ladies goodbye or maybe a stroll around the gardens?"

He turned and winked at Iris. "I'll see you at dinner." Her mouth fell open as her father strode out without saying more, leaving the four at the table. Iris's gaze moved to Laurel, whom John kissed on the cheek as she giggled.

Alex offered his hand to her as he rose. "A stroll, Mi'Lady?"

Laurel stood up. "She can't."

She turned to John. "We can't. I had her mother send the carriage."

Laurel eyed Iris. "We must go to the merchant for the rest of your costume." Her focus moved between the men. "The ball's next weekend and Iris's costume isn't finished." She leaned into John. "You are coming, aren't you?"

John tickled her as he replied. "Wouldn't miss it for the world. You said Lord Erskine permits you to attend in costume. Which costume shall I look for, sweetie?"

Laurel giggled. "You must find yer Scottish lass among the crowd."

Alex froze. "Lord Erskine is permitting ye to attend. Will yer cousin attend as well?"

Laurel's gaze landed on Iris. "I don't know. I haven't asked her yet."

Iris stood and turned to leave. This had to end soon, or she'd certainly expose herself as Ivy. This was too soon. She needed to gather herself and figure this out.

Alex turned to her and offered his hand. "Then this is goodbye, for now. I will see ye at the ball?"

Iris smiled and placed her hand in his. "Of that, you can be certain."

He rubbed his thumb over the back. *"Cò ris a chuireas tu aodach? Mar sin, is dòcha gum faigh mi thu?"* What will you dress as? So, I may find ye?

Feeling playful, Iris replied, *"A bhanrigh."* A queen.

Alex grinned wide. *"Gu ruige sin, mo bhanrigh."* Till then, my queen.

Chapter 9

Christmas morning came bright and cold with freshly fallen snow. A white Christmas usually excited Iris, but she didn't have that extra holiday spirit this year.

As Mabe, the scullery maid filling in for Laurel, tightened her stays Iris called out, "A little looser, please." When Mabe loosened the strings, Iris took a deep breath.

Christmas day. What would Alex be doing? Laurel had Christmas Eve plus the day off and planned on spending her free time with John at Alex's townhome. She promised to return this evening with a full accounting of all they'd done. Iris even sent a present for Alex, a Gaelic poem book. One that she favored holding poems on romance and the dreamy life of a Scot. She hoped he liked it. She certainly did.

Mabe touched her shoulder. "It's time to go downstairs, Mi'Lady. Yer parents wait with the presents." Iris nodded without comment and moved out the door, then down the stairs, with Mabe following.

The maid's chatter filled the void. "Imagine a Christmas tree. It's the first one I've seen, Miss. The pretty baubles that glitter in the candlelight. Why 'tis magical."

Each year, she and her parents exchanged presents for Christmas. Typically, her mother gave her gloves and her father a dress. She always gave her mother a hat and her father some of his favored cigars.

Mabe's chatter broke into her thoughts. "And the gift yer family gave the maids, why, it's the best pair of gloves I've ever owned. And with the fresh snow, I'll have them on when I head home later."

As for her gifts to her parents, this year, she veered a little off her normal course and opted to purchase Laurel's friend's linen. For her father, five handkerchiefs, and her mother, a scarf of the finer fabric. Iris felt a sense of pride supporting someone's business. The friend, Shay, was outright pleased with Iris's purchase. With her other orders, she'd moved her weaving loom to a warehouse and hired helpers to raise her production and sell to merchants. She'd boasted of the possibility of sending her first order to America soon. Iris was pleased to be a part of it.

As she stepped off the last stair, Iris turned to the parlor, where the newest addition to their Christmas decorations stood. Her mother saw one at a friend's house and insisted she must have one for them. A German tradition that Iris had to admit was, as Mabe had said, glittering balls that hung among the burning candles placed carefully on the evergreen tree in the corner of the room beside the fireplace.

Her mother bustled over and hugged her. "Iris, you look lovely, and Happy Christmas, darling."

She hugged her back. "And to you, mother."

Her father rose from his chair before the fire. "Right, so, and Happy Christmas." As soon as her mother let go, he stepped forward and kissed her on the cheek. When he pulled back, he winked at her.

Her mother, now totally in her element, host to a party, clapped her hands. "Presents!"

Iris and her father sat in the chairs before the fire as her mother selected wrapped boxes from under the tree passing them out to each recipient. She sat on the settee adjacent to them as each opened their gifts. Iris opened her present wrapped in decorative paper topped with mistletoe.

As Iris held up a brocade bag tied with silk rope, her mother beamed. "It's from both of us—a reticule. Well, that was what they called it. You carry your items inside and tie the bag to your side."

Her father opened her present to him and held the handkerchiefs up. "Why, thank you, Iris. A very thoughtful gift." He set them down still holding one in his hand as his fingers rubbed the fabric. "Such a fine weave as well. Nice and tight."

Iris leaned toward him. "Yes, hand-woven by a crafter here in Glasgow. I had your initials embroidered."

Her father gazed at her. "Thank you, Iris." She warmed at his soft tone that hinted at sincerity.

Her mother called out. "My turn to open Iris's gift!" She ripped the paper open like a child at first Christmas, and the linen scarf fell onto her lap. "Oh, Iris, this is beautiful." Her mother tossed the paper aside and held up the delicate fabric. "Iris, thank you, dear." She wrapped the material around herself. "Was this made by the same woman who made your father's handkerchiefs?" As her mother's expectant expression met hers she nodded.

Her mother rose and crossed to hug her, then stood holding her hand. "Iris, I owe you an apology. About Lieutenant Tytler." Her mother and father exchanged glances as her mother sat on the chair arm. "I didn't know all the horrible things he did. I truly thought him honorable." She sighed. "Your father will escort you to the Hogmanay Ball, and I hope you make the rounds dancing with all the eligible bachelors." Really, she only wanted to dance with one, Alex. She didn't care much for the others but looked forward to speaking to Alex as herself and seeing if he liked her as Iris.

Her father cleared his throat. "Yes, well, we had lunch with Alex MacDougall. He's quite a fine gentleman." Iris's face heated as she looked down.

Her mother smiled at her father. "He's your assistant of sorts, isn't he?" Her mother wiggled her hand. "And by the blush staining your cheeks, you enjoyed yourself with him."

Iris shrugged. "He is very nice and handsome." What would they say if they truly knew how much she liked Alex? Her mother loathed anyone Scottish, but she seemed to take a turn for approval. Would she approve of her and Alex? Iris hoped so with all her heart.

Her mother stood, releasing her hand. "Wonderful! Let's rest till dinner. Iris, gather your presents and take them to your room."

Iris rose and collected her items. "Thank you both and Happy Christmas."

Iris whiled away the afternoon with a Gaelic book, reading the same passage over and over as she impatiently waited for Laurel to return and tell her all about Christmas at Alex's home. Dinner came and went without much fanfare for Iris but a lot for her mother. Served for dinner was the typical Christmas menu of prime rib, Yorkshire pudding, braised red cabbage, and roasted chestnuts with Brussels sprouts. A brandied cranberry sauce accompanied the dishes well, and the white wine tasted fresh and light. Dessert was another holiday staple: plum pudding. Iris sat up well into the evening, trying to stay awake for when Laurel came home, but with her belly full and the night waning. Her eyelids dropped, and she nodded off.

****

Bright sunlight woke Iris as Laurel's voice filled her room. "Ye sleepy head! Ye slept in yer clothes!"

Iris sat bolt upright, startled from her slumber. "What time is it?"

Her maid pulled back the rest of the bed curtains securing them to the posts. "Near midday already. I slept in myself and didn't return to the manor until a little while ago."

Iris jumped from the bed and followed Laurel to her armoire as she dug through it. "Well?"

Laurel's reply sounded muffled in the clothing. "Nothing much." She pulled out a sturdy wool dress and held the garment up. "It snowed again. It's damned cold out." Her maid laid the gown on the bed, pulled out a drawer, and dug through it, adding woolen stockings.

Iris crossed and stood before her maid. "Tell me all. I want to know everything." Laurel set the stockings down and smiled at her.

She pulled a note from her bodice and waved the parchment before Iris. "Why don't ye see for yerself."

Iris's eyes went wide. A letter! On the front of the paper in a scrawling script was one word *Ivy*. Finally, a letter from Alex she could hold and read.

She grabbed the note and crossed to the window for better light to read by. She flipped the paper over, and the red wax seal was an *M* with interwoven vines. *M* for MacDougall. Iris ran her finger under the seal, and the stamp popped, leaving the wax intact. She opened the letter, reading the clean script.

My dearest Ivy,

I hope your Christmas was as joyful as mine. Laurel, John, and I missed you for Christmas dinner. The good news is that Mabina sent too much food. Please join me for a second Christmas dinner this evening, just the two of us.

Thank you for the Christmas gift. I enjoyed the Gaelic poetry book. Come this evening, and I shall give you your gift then. I hope you will treasure my gift.

Laurel will get word to me. Please say yes and allow me to share my holiday with you.

Yours truly, Alex.

Iris hugged the letter to her chest, twirled, and landed on her bed, crumpling the dress and stockings.

She groaned as Laurel pushed her aside. "Ye're crushing yer dress, and from the look on yer face combined with the sigh, I suspect yer response will be aye."

Iris sat up. "How do you say Merry Christmas in Gaelic?"

Laurel brushed the dress out. "*Nollaig Chridheil* means Merry Christmas. You could also say *Nollaig Chridheil agus Bliadhna Mhath Ùr,* which means Merry Christmas and a Happy New Year."

Iris tried the words out as Laurel stripped off her day-old clothing. "*Nollaig Chridheil*" She held the letter as they maneuvered the clothing.

Laurel pulled her clean dress over her head, forcing her to switch the letter from hand to hand. She wasn't letting her Highlander's note go.

Iris glanced up at Laurel. "Tell me all that you did."

Laurel laughed. "And spoil Alex's surprise? Not a

chance, *Ivy*. Ye must wait and find out for yerself." Iris dressed and sat at the window as she practiced the Gaelic words until they flowed from her lips.

Her maid sent word to Alex via a stable boy; the reply was, "*Gu ar n-àm, a ghràidh.*"

After Laurel spoke the words, Iris translated them quickly, "Till our time… Oh, damn, what's the last one?"

Laurel rolled her eyes. "Till our time, darling."

All too soon, yet not soon enough, Laurel led Iris, dressed in her wool riding dress and a borrowed black cloak, through the kitchens and into the stable yard. Mac stood in the cold with their saddled horses waiting for the ladies to arrive.

As Mac gave Iris a leg up on Pixie, her father rode into the stable yard. When Iris gained the saddle, she snapped upright. Laurel mounted as their gazes connected. He couldn't stop her from going. She waited all day yesterday through today to see Alex.

Her father dismounted and strode toward them. "A bit late for a ride, ladies." His face tilted to the sky. "Looks like more snow." When his head came down, his eyes met Iris's, and his eyebrow lifted. "Iris, where's your new cloak? The blue one?"

Iris gathered the reins in her hands. "In the wash. Nonsense, Father, we're off on an errand." She kneed Pixie into a trot before her father could reply.

At the turn into the lane, Laurel caught up with her. "Thank ye. Ye left me to deal with yer da. He said not to be out too late."

Iris shrugged and rode on toward High Street. They made their way through the town to the other side without incident, and soon, Iris rode into Alex's stable yard.

She dismounted with no one to greet her, and Laurel soon followed. "Ye will be the death of me, Iris." She murmured, "I'll come to get ye around midnight."

Iris uttered back, "And what if I don't want to come home yet?"

Laurel's eyes went wide as she hissed. "Ye're a lady. An innocent." Iris took her mount into the stable to undo the saddle.

Something she was glad Mac insisted she learn on her own, saying, "Anyone who learned how to ride had to learn to tack their own horse."

Laurel followed. "If he takes yer innocence, I'm done for if yer mother finds out."

Iris pulled the saddle down and set the heavy tack aside as she whispered, "I just want to spend more time with him. Nothing will happen."

Laurel huffed. "Says the fly flying into the spider's web." Iris put the saddle blanket on the saddle and led Pixie to a stall. As the horse went inside, she removed the harness and patted her rear before closing the gate.

When she turned, Alex stood in the doorway. "Ye came." He strode toward her. "Ye arrived early. I planned on meeting ye in the yard and stabling yer horse." He pulled a blanket from a shelf and placed the wool over Pixie, who neighed softly in response.

Iris shook her head as Alex took her hands in his. "I gave the staff a couple of days off."

He glanced at Laurel. "Laurel, I wasn't aware ye were coming. John's gone home to visit family while I'm stuck with court cases." He huffed a laugh. "The court doesn't take off for the holiday."

Laurel shook her head. "No, just seeing Ivy here." Her gaze narrowed to Iris. "I'll be back, Ivy."

Iris nodded, and when Alex turned, she mouthed, "Tomorrow, sunrise."

Alex pulled her along, and Iris willingly followed. When they entered the back door, Alex removed her cloak. As he passed, she handed over her gloves.

He took her hands in his and rubbed them. "Come, there's mulled wine, and we'll warm ye by the fire." He took her through the kitchens, where an assortment of foods warmed over the fire.

She paused, eyeing the spread, and he chuckled. "Dinner later. Wine and warmth first, Ivy." She followed him through the entry to the parlor, where a fire roared. Alex situated her before the fireplace, and her gaze roamed the room. Holly and ivy decorated the mantel and nearly every surface. The side tables even had a small, tied sprig on each.

He returned to her side and handed her a wine glass filled with dark red wine. As she lifted it, the scent of spices wafted to her. When she sipped the rich wine, cinnamon and cloves tickled her tastebuds. She kept her back to the fire, grateful for its warmth. Alex stepped forward and held her in his arms as she snuggled into his embrace. They stood there silently in each other's arms.

Alex hummed. "I've wanted to hold ye each and every day since the last time, Ivy." He moved back, keeping her in his arms as his eyes traveled over her face, then her hair that she'd left folded under a braid to the side. His free hand brushed her cheek and then fingered her hair, which reflected red in the firelight.

He bent and kissed her. "*Nollaig Chridheil.*" She mouthed the words to him, and he smiled. Iris turned in his arms and pointed to the holly and ivy on the mantel, then the tables.

When her eyes found his, he chuckled. "A tradition from my mother. She decorates everything for the holidays. Evergreens and mistletoe cover nearly every surface that will hold it." He glanced around the room. "I guess the decoration makes me feel closer to home. It's my first time away over the holidays, and I admit, I miss it." His eyes connected with hers. "I chose holly and ivy since the greenery reminded me of when we met." Iris stepped out of his embrace and lifted her glass to him. She waved around, hoping to indicate a new home.

When her eyes came around to meet his, he lifted an eyebrow. "A toast. To what, Ivy?" She waved her hand around the room again, then pointed to the holly and ivy.

Alex nodded and held his glass out. "Aye, a toast to new traditions." They clinked their glasses and took a sip, holding each other's gaze over the rims. Alex took her glass and set hers down with his, then held her hand as he led her out of the room back into the kitchen. He picked up a large wooden plate likely used for the servants' meals. She giggled without sound as he grabbed a cloth, leaned into the cooking fire, and hefted one pot then another placing them on the table. With a grin, he lifted each lid, revealing the remains of a hearty meal. Roast goose sat sliced over oat dressing with bits of dates. Next to it were roasted potatoes and parsnips.

Alex handed her a fork. "Dig in, lass. There's enough here for more than ye and me."

She forked a slice of goose on the single plate he held, then a scoop of stuffing and moved on to the potatoes placing some on the plate.

Alex reached across her and using the cloth he picked up a smaller pot from the fire. "Here, lass, ye need gravy for the stuffing and goose." He held the vessel out, and Iris nodded as he poured a bit over each. She moved to a tray lifting the cloth and stuffed rolls sat before her. She bent and sniffed smelling sausage. Alex grabbed one, stuffing the pastry in his mouth as he hummed.

He spoke as he chewed. "Mabina's haggis rolls." He chewed some more. "Melts in yer mouth."

Iris had never had haggis. She'd heard about it. Most English refused to eat sheep's entrails, yet the scent was of spicey sausage. She picked one up and bit into it. The flaky crust reminded her of sausage rolls, but she rolled the bits around when the meat hit her mouth, testing the texture. When she chewed, sage and other spices hit her tongue. The roll was really quite good. She took another and placed the pastry on her plate. Alex placed more on the plate as she stood back and waited. He grabbed two cloths and led her back to the parlor. She paused at the door and glanced toward the darkened dining room.

Alex entered the parlor and stood before the fire. "Lass, join me here where it's warm." He pulled the end table closer and set the stand between each chair.

He waved to the other chair as he set the plate on the table. "Mi'Lady."

She crossed and sat in the chair, and Alex took her glass and filled it. This was more comfortable than dining chairs. When she raised her head, Alex stood before her with her wine.

He handed the glass to her and sat beside her. "At Dunstaffnage Castle, my home in Argyle, we dine in a great hall. My mother and father sit side by side, sharing a plate. The habit comes from when they were first married, and he caught a cousin poisoning her food over a clan feud."

Iris gasped, and Alex caught her hand before it came

to her chest. "Not to worry—it all ended well. But the sharing of a trencher, they still honor." He brought her hand to his lips and kissed the back. "It's a tradition I'd like to continue with the woman I am fond of. I hope ye don't mind."

Sharing a plate was such a simple thing—yet as Alex started cutting the goose, she found sitting like this, close and intimate. He forked a perfect portion of goose with stuffing and offered her a bite. She took a bite and her face warmed as he filled his fork again and ate, then took another forkful as she chewed. He offered her another taste, this time of potatoes.

Alex took another two forkfuls and spoke as he chewed. "I had planned on going home to visit my family, but it seems the courts will not honor Daft Days." Daft Days, she'd not heard of it.

Iris must have given him a questioning expression because he blew a laugh when he glanced at her. "Daft Days are the days between Christmas and New Year for celebrating." He smiled as he stared into the fire. "My parents call it yule time as in the old tradition. My da still insists on finding a large yule log to bring in and burn the entire holiday." Alex's gaze moved to hers. "They still decorate it. It's a ceremony my family observes."

He set the fork down and sat forward, his hands forming a long, round shape. "They present the log before the clan, and each family member places an item on top that burns with the log for luck for the new year." His hands rested in his lap. "My ma, she always places a sprig of mistletoe on the log." His eyes met hers. "She keeps a mistletoe sprig for herself, to kiss under for Hogmanay, for luck." The echo of his first asking if he could kiss her came to her mind, and her eyes landed on his lips.

He leaned over toward her. "A kiss, Ivy?" She nodded slightly as his lips captured hers. Their tongues danced, and she felt a little lightheaded. He ended the kiss and sat back as he picked up his glass and sipped. She leaned back and took a sip from hers as well. The heady wine cleared her head a little from the kiss.

Alex hummed as he picked up the fork again. "We must finish dinner. I have more planned for this night." After a few more bites, Iris rested back and sighed.

Her host finished off the plate and picked up the plate and utensil. "I'll be back with dessert."

He disappeared into the kitchen, and Iris sat sipping her wine, watching the flames of the fire. Dining from the same plate was such an intimate act. Alex fed her the entire meal, almost knowing what she wanted and when. She grinned to herself. Alex was such a caring man.

A bowl with a spoon appeared before her, and she gasped. Alex stood behind her, his breath tickling her ear. "Clootie dumpling."

She reached for the spoon, but he pulled the offering away and set the utensil on the table. "Ah, but you'll be needing something to help the cake go down easier."

She held her wine glass out. He took her cup but didn't fill it. He set that on the table as well. Intrigued, she sat forward to turn around, and his hand on her shoulder stopped her.

As he knelt beside her, his breath came to her ear again. "I have yer Christmas gift, Ivy."

He placed a small, wrapped package in her hands. The red paper offset the green sprig of mistletoe tied in the bow on top. Iris carefully slid the ribbon off the box so the bow held the mistletoe tightly. She set that aside as she glanced at Alex. He watched her hands intently. She paused, staring at his profile, relaxed with a tilt to his smile. She reached up to his cheek and brushed her hand down the side. His gaze rose and met hers.

He took her hand and kissed the inner wrist, then placed it back on the box. "Open yer gift. I had this made special for ye." Iris gasped, and as she looked at the box, she ripped the paper open like a child, excited to see the surprise waiting inside.

Alex chuckled and kissed her cheek. When she opened the carton and pulled away the soft fabric, a silver long box sat inside. The carvings on the outside were ivy vines with leaves sprouting from side to side. She picked the box up, and as she turned it, the vines continued in one long strand, never-ending. She held the silver item up when she noted a screw top.

Her focus went to Alex, then back to the box. No, wait, not a box. Iris set down the container the gift came in and unscrewed the lid. When she peeked inside, the scent of rich whisky wafted to her nose.

When it dawned on her what she held, she turned and faced Alex who gave her a wide grin. "Aye, lass. A woman's flask made just for ye."

Iris took a sip, swished the flavorful liquor in her mouth, took a deep breath, and then swallowed the potent drink. She moaned and screwed the lid back on as Alex hummed.

As she sat forward, she grabbed her newest gift from her parents, her reticule. She pulled open the strings, dropped her small flask inside, and pulled her bag shut.

Alex grunted. "What, will ye not share?" Iris shook her head and patted her bag. Alex stood and handed her the bowl, but she pushed the dessert back to him.

He stood staring at her. "Ye don't want the dumpling?" She shook her head again, and he turned to set the bowl on the table. She grabbed his wrist and pulled him to the floor at her feet.

Alex followed slowly, seeming uncertain of what she wanted. When he stopped in a kneeling position, she pushed on his shoulders until he sat at her feet. She pointed to the dumpling and then the spoon and slowly brought her finger to her lips.

When a devilish smile crossed Alex's face, she knew he understood what she wanted. He scooted forward a bit and sat up on his haunches till his elbow rested on the chair's arm. He spooned some of the cake and offered the dessert to her. She wrapped her lips around the spoon, taking a bite.

Never taking his eyes from hers, he lifted a portion of cake and wrapped his lips around the serving, eating the dessert. Upon each dollop, Alex moved to her.

They moved closer until he brushed his lips against hers. The spices of the cake mingled between their breaths as he tilted his head so his lips could devour hers. So caught up in the sensual sensations, Iris let a little moan escape. Alex set the bowl aside and took her head in his hands as his lips traveled to her ear, sending bolts of heat rushing through her. He pulled back a little, and she moved forward, falling off the seat into his arms.

Alex pulled her over him till their bodies came flush against one another as his lips connected with hers again. He rolled her to his side, and his hand slid over her breast, sending tingles over her body. First hot, then cold as she shivered with desire. His kisses traveled down her neck to the top of her breasts, and she arched into his embrace. His tongue trailed along the edge of her bodice, and she let a moan slip.

Alex raised his head and kissed her lips hard. "Ivy, I want so badly to show ye how much I… I…"

Her fingers threaded through his hair, the queue in the back coming undone, allowing his waves to fall to his shoulders. She pulled his lips to hers and kissed him thoroughly, hoping she conveyed her emotions in the one kiss. She wanted to shout aloud that she loved him and wanted to show him her heart, but as Ivy, she couldn't utter a word. Alex pulled away and rested his forehead against hers, panting as he did so. She brushed her hand over his cheek, lifting his face till their eyes met. She tilted her eyebrows, trying to plead with him, wanting to say, *please love me, Alex.*

He must have read her mind, for he sat back and took her into his arms. "Ivy, I wish to show ye my heart this night." He lifted her as he stood, easily carrying her weight. "I wish to show ye the man I am, the feelings I share with ye. Please tell me ye wish the same."

Tears gathered in her eyes. He'd read her mind and her heart. Iris nodded as she laid her hand on his heart, then hers, telling him she shared his feelings. Alex brushed a kiss on her lips as he slowly walked across the room into the hall. He moved on the first stair, not taking his eyes off her, and tripped on the second.

She stifled a giggle as he huffed. "I'd best watch where I step, or we'll both end up in a heap on the floor."

Chapter 10

They cleared the top step without incident, and Alex strode to the end of the hallway. He elbowed into his room, and the fire burned lowly, casting the room in a familiar red glow. He moved past the table beside the chair they'd slept in before and lowered her to stand beside the bed.

Alex bent and kissed her, his hands roaming her bodice. "Ivy, ye do know what will happen. Between us, I mean…"

She pulled back from his kiss with a grin on her face. He hesitated, making her smile. While a virgin, she was not innocent of the ways between man and woman. His concern touched her more than he could ever know. Alex was a man who allowed her independent thoughts of a woman and valued her traditional views of love. She moved from his embrace and turned away as she took another few steps. Iris glanced at him over her shoulder, noticing he'd gone still—eyes wide, lips slightly parted, breath held. The transfixed look on his face told her everything: he was too awestruck to speak caught in mute wonder.

She pulled on her bodice ties, loosening the knot, then unlaced the strings. Alex moved to her, and she rotated and put her hand against his chest, shaking her head. She pushed him to the bed till he sat. Iris patted his chest, then moved back. When she angled away and glanced over her shoulder again to see if he watched, he chuckled deeply in his throat.

Iris pulled on the strings again until the bodice came fully loose. When she moved to face Alex, he shifted onto the bed, laying back with his hands crossed behind his head. Her face warmed as she held her bodice in place, still covering her breasts. Good, he understood the game she wished to play.

Iris lowered her bodice slowly, and the rush of cold air gave her a shiver. Or was it Alex's hooded gaze? Allowing the bodice to drop, Iris turned again and untied her overshirt, allowing the fabric to slip to the floor slowly as she kept her back to him. She stepped from the garment and lifted her foot, resting it on the bed frame. She flipped her shift back, exposing her full leg as Alex growled. She made quick work of her shoelaces and flipped her shoe off, letting the item clatter on the floor. She repeated the same for the other foot, and Alex shifted on the bed in a groan.

Iris twisted to face him as she stepped closer, untying the laces of her shift. With each move she took closer, the undergarment loosened and fell from her shoulders. Her hands on her breasts were the only thing keeping the garment on her body. As she came alongside him, she lifted her hands to her shoulders letting the fabric slip off her body as her arms lowered, baring herself to him. His eyes roamed her form, then rushed to her face.

As he rose from the bed, he muttered, "God, ye are lovely." He took her into his arms, pulling her over him onto the bed. Alex's body covered hers as his hands slid up her sides to her breasts, cupping them as he kissed her deeply.

Her hands moved over his back as his hands and lips wreaked havoc on her senses. When his kisses moved to her throat, then her breasts as heat spread to her core. Tingles spread through her as his lips latched onto a nipple and suckled. Her fists grabbed his jacket front and yanked the garment open.

Alex rose above her with a smirk on his face. "Ivy, are ye trying to tell me I have too many clothes on?" Her eyes met his, and her hands slid under his shirt, her face set in grim determination.

He grabbed her wrists and held them as he smiled. "My mother always told my father, all's fair in love and war." He kissed one hand and released them as he slid off the bed. She sat up, reaching for him, but he moved back and shook his head. Alex stood tall and straightened his shirt and coat, pulling them down covering him. Was he teasing her? She grinned, loving his playful nature. As he pulled on his coat sleeve and removed one arm, she sat up and leaned on one hand. Her other hand reached for her hair, pulling out the pins one by one. Alex's eyes followed her movement, and he stripped his coat from his body. She reached over and set her hairpins on the nightstand, and when she turned back, he pulled his shirt over his head. When his face met hers, she ran her fingers through her braid, releasing her hair, and moved the curls over her chest. As Alex unbuttoned his trews, he took a step toward her.

Iris lounged back against the pillows, allowing her hair to cover most of the best parts of her body. Alex growled as he kicked off his boots. On the next step, he stripped his pants down and kicked them off. He came to her, his body gloriously naked and beautiful. Muscles undulated as he crawled onto the bed and covered her.

Alex ran his fingers through her hair to the ends that tickled the apex of her legs. He trailed his fingers to her garters holding her stockings up, and untied one. He bent and ran kisses from her hip to her knee as he pulled one off. Alex pressed her side, turning her, and repeated the same for the other leg. Laying exposed before him as she had to no one else, she shivered and started to cover herself.

Alex took hold of her hands. "No, I wish to see all of ye."

He bent and kissed her full on the mouth whispering into the kiss. "I wish to worship all of ye."

Iris stopped her arms, and Alex released her hands, allowing him to move them over her breasts as he kissed her deeply. He rolled to her side, moving his hand down her body and covering her. Heat spread through her again as he pushed his hand on her, and something built within her. The same feeling she had the night they played in the chair. Alex slid a finger over her, and her legs fell open. His tongue delved into her mouth in the same pattern as his finger moved on her body, and a rising sensation overcame her. He sped up his pace, and heat flashed over her again—the pressure built as she panted. Alex kissed her harder as his hand kept moving, pushing her to an unknown place she so desperately wanted to go. Iris arched her back and bit her lip to keep herself from calling out. The pressure climbed as his hand continued its sweet torture. He slid a finger inside her, and her world broke apart in a deep groan. Moisture spread over her, and a wave consumed her.

Alex shifted and rolled over her as he took her head in his hands. "Ivy, please, I must have ye." He kissed her as he rubbed himself against her, spreading the moisture between them. He moved closer, his hips spreading her legs wide, opening herself to him. He rubbed against her again as he kissed her. He flexed his hips, and the tip of him slid into her.

He froze and locked gazes with her. "It will hurt a little. For that, I am sorry. But I promise the rest will be ecstasy." His hand came to her cheek, and he slid in a little more, stretching her to take him. Sweat broke out on his forehead as he bent to brush his lips lightly against hers.

Iris wanted all of him, all he had to give. She grabbed his hips and pulled hard. He took her cue and drove into her, keeping his lips locked with hers.

The burning pain rocked her, and she must have moaned because Alex kissed her as he whispered shushes. His fingers wiped tears that had escaped, and he kissed her again as he held himself still.

Iris returned his kisses. The receding pain fast became replaced with a fullness she enjoyed. His large body covered hers, pressing her into the bedding. Iris felt conquered. He shifted, and she kissed him. He pulled out a little, then slid back in, and heat flushed her again. Her hands moved over his back and to his shoulders, encouraging him.

As Alex kissed her and moved again, she felt his lips curve with a gentle shift in pressure that seemed to be a smile, and his reaction put one on her lips. He took her signal well and began a steady rhythm that returned the enjoyable pressure. Her hands roamed his body, first his back flexing with each thrust into her, then over his shoulders that contracted as he moved. She moved them to his chest, as he rose a little, gaining better leverage to thrust himself into her. His hand trailed from her neck to her breast. He cupped and kneaded with each push his body made.

Now more accustomed to his size and movement, Iris tried meeting each thrust with one of her own. On the second push, he growled lowly and bent to kiss her hard. His thrusts came faster as he rested his elbows on either side of her face. That pressure built as she panted heavily. Iris had to bite her lip again to stop her from screaming his name as she arched into him, lights exploded behind her eyelids, and the damn broke.

As she still rode the wave of pleasure, Alex quickened his movements, drove into her once, then again, and shouted, "Ivy."

He shook as he froze over her, rolled to the side, pulled her to him, and cradled her in his arms. The wrong name, but she understood the sentiment. In a way, she was Ivy and Iris, both at once. They both lay there panting as their sweat cooled their bodies. At first, the room spun for Iris, but once she controlled her breathing, she gained her wits again.

Alex trailed his fingers up and down her arm, and a chill washed over her, bringing out a shiver. He sat up and reached toward the end of the bed, pulling a blanket that matched his tartan over them. She curled into his embrace, resting her head against his chest, wishing this could be where she fell asleep and woke every day for the rest of her life.

The bed shifted, waking her. Alex took her in his arms again and held a cup for her to drink. "Ale, cool and will wet yer whistle." She drank deeply. He was right. Their activities had left her parched. He stretched to set the cup on the nightstand, then returned and held her close to his heart. She ran her fingers through his springy chest hair, loving the feeling of them naked together.

Alex hummed and squeezed her once. "Ivy. Lord Erskine is having a ball for New Year." She froze at the mention of her father's name. She knew he'd invited Alex. She had made plans to be with him as Iris, hoping he'd like her as herself.

He tilted till he gazed into her eyes. "It's a costumed ball. I'm going to wear my plaid. Please be my escort and come as a Scottish lady." He blew a laugh. "We could yell the MacDougall battle cry. *Buaidh No Bas. Victory or Death*, startling everyone." Her eyes went wide, and she shook her head.

Alex brushed her cheek with the back of his hand. "Please. It would make me the happiest of men." She lay down and shook her head again.

Alex huffed. "Why not? Laurel is permitted to attend. Why not ye?" Iris sighed. How could she explain her predicament to him? *I'm really Iris. I've lied to you for a while, but please forgive me. I did it because I love you.* No, this wasn't so easy. Iris lifted her hands and used her fingers to indicate many as she wiggled them.

Alex's head went back into the pillow. "Ye must be the willow in the breeze?"

She dropped her hands on his chest, making him jolt. "I tease. I understand. Ye must be with family." What she communicated wasn't an outright lie, but the fib burned her conscience all the same. She wanted to express who she was, but only after Alex had the same feelings for Iris that he had for Ivy.

Her throat closed as her nose burned. Tears gathered quickly in her eyes, and she took a breath, trying to stop them. The air came in more like a hiccup, and a tear escaped and landed on Alex's bare chest.

He turned and took her face in his hands. "Tears? Oh, lass. Please don't cry. I didn't ask ye to make ye sad. I wanted to share the holiday with ye, be with ye." He wiped her face with his thumb as more tears fell at his declaration. What she wouldn't give just to be able to tell him all and not have this hurt him, hurt them.

He tucked her into his embrace. "Shh. Calm yerself, Ivy. Let me tell ye a bedtime fable. One my ma told me as a child." He kissed her head, "Rest and listen, lass."

"There was a prince who lived in the castle. The Fae gifted him with the Stone of Love. The stone was very powerful, and the Fae charged him with guarding it. He made a necklace for the heart-shaped stone and always wore the gem so that he would know when his true love was near because then, the stone would glow red." Iris glanced at him, her eyebrows lifted.

Alex grinned. "Aye, the stone glowed for his true love." He patted her back, and she settled into his embrace, looking forward to a fairy story of magic and whimsy.

His chest vibrated as he began the tale again. "Many maidens came from far and wide to see if the stone would glow for them, but the gem never did. The prince became depressed, thinking he'd never find his true love. He sneaked away to the village to sit at his favorite spot by the stream and contemplate the issue with the stone. The gem would glow whenever he went to the stream, but he was always alone." Iris trailed her fingers in his chest hair, wishing for a magic stone to tell Alex of her feelings and her identity and make this all right.

Alex paused and took a deep breath. He squeezed her once, making her feel comfortable and safe. "One day, a beautiful woman came to the castle. Gorgeous and sensual, she went near him and made the stone glow. While physically attracted to her, the prince did not feel love for this woman. Confused, he snuck off to his spot by the stream. As he sat, he saw a maiden approached."

Alex turned to her and caressed her cheek. "She had glowing cream-colored skin and an inner beauty he had not seen in a woman before."

He dropped his hand and stared at the ceiling as he spoke. "Her light-brown hair glimmered in the sunlight, seeming as if to cast the threads of a pure gold halo around her head. Her soul called him in a way he had never felt before."

Alex tilted her chin till their eyes met. "The first day I saw ye. Yer red hair escaped yer cloak and cast ye in a halo." Iris felt a gentle rush that increased her heartbeat, recalling the day as well. But she also recalled he turned his back on her. Alex hummed, kissed her, and lay back, staring at the ceiling again. He took a deep breath and then another. She laid her cheek against his chest, and his heart hammered fast. What bothered him about the fable? Maybe he'd forgotten a part, and she shifted her hands out.

He grabbed them and kissed them. "Sorry, I lost myself in a memory. The fable."

He held her hands to his chest. "So caught up in his examination, he had not noticed that the Stone of Love glowed red." She smiled, liking this story. The simple maiden at the stream was the prince's true love. If only life were really so simple.

Alex took a deep breath. "The prince must have made a noise because the village girl turned startled, and she dropped her water bucket. Her face met his, and her shock was apparent. 'I'm sorry to disturb you, Prince.'

Her voice sounded as if the angels sang for him alone.

"The prince rose and retrieved her bucket, handing the pail to her, 'I'm sorry I surprised you.'

"The girl stared at the stone, pulsing red. The prince so caught up in the village girl's enchantment, only now noticed the stone glowed. Shocked, he took her to the castle to see if the stone glowed for both women." Iris froze when Alex mentioned two women. Did he place the detail there to tell her he knew she was really two women? Would he be angry if he found out? She held her breath as he continued the story, not noticing her distress.

His voice rose with his telling as his breaths came fast. "Upon arriving at the castle, he confronted the evil Fae. The Stone of Love burned his clothes and chest when he approached her. Angry that they discovered her secret, the evil Fae cast a spell upon the village girl and the prince, opening a portal to purgatory.

" 'True love or a lifetime in purgatory—choose yer fate,' she yelled at the prince.

"Confused, the prince asked, 'Why do you do this? Why do you hate so much?'

"The village girl answered for the evil Fae. 'She does not hate—she is fearful. The opposite of love is not hate, but *fear*.'

"The prince offered the stone from his neck to his true love, the maiden from the stream. 'I shall live forever in purgatory so ye may live a full life. Take the Stone of Love.' But her love for him was so strong that she could not allow the prince to sacrifice himself for her, the village girl. When he handed her the stone, she thrust the gem into his hands and jumped into the portal, casting herself into purgatory, and saving the prince."

Alex's voice rose again, and he flexed his arms, gripping her as he spoke. "So angered by this, the prince turned upon the evil Fae and drove his sword through her heart while holding the necklace with the Stone of Love in the same hand as the sword. The evil Fae's blood dripped from the blade to the Stone of Love. Dropping his sword to the ground, the prince fell to his knees, gripping the Stone of Love to his heart. He prayed to the Fae that his true love would return to him." Alex stopped and loosened his hold on her.

His voice took on an edge she'd not heard before. "Dagda, the king of the Tuatha Dé Dannan, appeared. 'I am sorry, prince, I cannot help ye. A spell cast by the evil Fae I cannot undo. But I can give ye a chant, and ye may call her back if yer love is powerful enough. But I warn ye, the chant will fail if she does not return yer love.' Roaring in his pain, the prince focused his prayer on his one true love. He chanted:

"I want to see love's highest power
Take me now, not to my past
Right now, at this hour,
Bring my true love back at last"

Alex nearly shouted the charm and stopped momentarily, his breath slowing.

When he spoke next, his voice sounded far away. "He prayed over and over. He closed his eyes and poured all his love into his one wish. The Stone of Love grew hot in his hand, so hot he had to let it go. The gem floated to the center of the room, hovering above everyone, and glowed pure white. The prince kept repeating his chant. The Stone of Love burst into a million points of light, blinding everyone momentarily. When their eyes adjusted, they saw the village girl standing in the center of the room."

Alex held her to his chest and shook a little. "Overcome with emotion, the prince threw his arms around her and kissed her. The sun shone through the glass window above them, casting them in a light halo.

"Dagda said to all in the room, 'The greatest power of all is true love.' " Iris turned to him, and a tear trailed down his cheek. She lifted her hand and brushed the droplet away with her fingertips.

Alex shook himself as if waking from a trance. "Sorry, lass. I'd forgotten how that fable affected me."

Iris shook her head, rose, and kissed him on the lips, trying to say, *it's okay. I understand.* The fable affected her as well. Two women loving one man—one evil, one not. She wasn't evil, but her betrayal felt like it. He kissed her back and stared at her. He sighed, and she laid her head back on his chest, listening to the steady beat of his heart.

****

Light snores woke Iris. The fire burned low, and a chill cast around the room. She glanced at the window and darkness showed dawn had not arrived. But the late hour told her the sun would soon. She slid from Alex's embrace, and his snores stopped. She froze. What would he do if he caught her sneaking away?

As his snores resumed, she slipped away. Iris stopped at the nightstand and quickly braided her hair, grabbing her pins and pinning them in a messy knot on the side of her head. She resumed her getaway by picking up her discarded garments one by one. Her shoes clunked against the polished wooden floor, but Alex still did not wake. Iris shivered from the cold and risked stopping to slip her shift over her head. Outside his door, she made quick work of her clothing. She left the stays a little loose knowing her cloak would cover it. Tiptoeing down the stairs, she found the bottom floor cast in darkness. Turning, she went into the kitchen, grabbed her cloak and gloves. The food from dinner was still out, and she snatched a few of the haggis rolls, shoving them in the cloak's pockets. The door squeaked when she opened it, and the knob shut with a loud click. Iris froze, waiting for someone to sound an alarm, but the silence of a cold night met her ears.

Upon entering the stable, Pixie greeted her with a grunt when she removed the warm cover and placed the saddle blanket and then the saddle on her. When she offered the bridle and bit, she took them easily. Maybe she understood Iris's need to be away quietly and quickly.

Iris ate a roll and then another, not knowing if she'd have the time or the stomach to eat one later. She needed to be home before sunrise to sneak into her home unnoticed.

The ride in the dark across town left an eerie feeling in her bones—as if she walked with the dead. No one was about. Nothing moved, not even a breeze. When she finally rounded the turn leading to her manor house, the sun peeked over the horizon, casting a purple-then-pink glow. When she came into the stable yard, Laurel exited the manor. They both froze as if caught in a criminal act.

Laurel blew her breath. "Damn it, Iris."

She slid from Pixie's back, and Mac appeared at her side. The three said nothing, and nothing would be repeated. Iris buried her head into her cloak as Laurel steered her through the empty kitchens into the home, up the stairs, and into her bedroom. She undressed unaided as Laurel stood by the door. A tear fell, and she wiped the drop away.

When she climbed into her bed, Laurel came and tucked her in. "It's hard, I know. Loving a man ye ought not. But ye do with all yer heart." Laurel was right. She loved Alex MacDougall with all her heart. If only he'd love Iris.

****

Alex woke as Bertha built up the fire in his room. He glanced around finding no sign of Ivy. He started to rise, and the room's chill quickly reminded him of his undressed state.

He folded his plaid over him as he addressed his housekeeper. "Bertha, did ye see anyone this morning when ye came in?"

She rose, dusting her hands off. "No, but I found yer mess ye left in my kitchen. Hope ye enjoyed yer feast. I ate the rest of the haggis rolls as yer penalty for messing up my area." Alex sat there full and well, knowing he'd spent the evening with Ivy. His body certainly felt the residuals of their evening play. Bertha bustled about his room, tidying up by picking up his discarded clothing.

She huffed at his coat and folded it. "Will said to tell ye don't leave the stable door open in the cold. The horses will freeze." He hadn't, but he had a good idea who had. Ivy. In her haste to flee him, she'd likely left the gate open. Why would she need to sneak away, and what secrets did she hold? Ivy perplexed Alex, and he vowed to get to the bottom of it. But he needed to rise for now—no *daft days* for him. A day at court was on his schedule today.

Chapter 11

Iris stood beside her father as her mother greeted another guest. Standing in the foyer was not how she'd expected to spend her evening at a ball, yet she played the dutiful daughter at her mother's insistence that they greet the guests. Her eye caught her reflection in the entryway mirror. The white wig did a perfect job hiding her auburn hair, and the malachite powder the shop owner sold her reflected off the mask that covered most of her face. She tilted her head again, and the silver flashed in the light from the hundreds of candles her mother insisted they needed.

Her father's greeting caught her attention. "Lieutenant Tytler, so good of you to join us this evening." She turned, and the English officer smiled as he shook her father's hand.

Her father laughed. "No costume or are you a *squabby* tonight?"

The Lieutenant stiffened at the comment replying in a curt tone, "Death or glory, my lord." He marched before her and bowed. Iris curtsied but did not offer her hand. His eyes went down, then back to her face. She gripped her hands hard, preventing them from fidgeting under his scrutiny. His gaze roamed her costume, and when his eyes returned to her face, he raised an eyebrow.

He glared at her as he spoke in a clipped tone. "The white hair doesn't become you. The color makes you look older."

Iris fingered the wig. "It's part of the costume. I like it."

His eyes stayed on her face. "A mythical creature for sure, but what are you this evening, I— My Lady?" He'd started to use her given name, but as her father cleared his throat, he switched to a more formal address.

She twisted, showing him her wings. "Will you not hazard a guess?" The next man in line spoke before Lieutenant Tytler could reply.

His familiar, deep voice sent chills through Iris. "A queen. Titania, queen of the fairies."

When she turned, Alex stood beside the Lieutenant dressed in full Highland Regalia. A sizeable decorative pin held his clean, bright red tartan over a dark blue waistcoat. His knees flexed as he shifted his weight between his feet and his socks folded over his knee-high boots. Iris suspected this was no costume but the formal wear of his clan. The image he presented made her knees weak.

Iris clapped her hands. "You are quite right, Mr. MacDougall." She offered her hand to him. He took her palm and bowed over her, lightly kissing the back. She'd not worn gloves, and his lips, soft and warm, sent sparks up her arm.

The Lieutenant stepped aside. "Titania? I have not heard of this person. Who is she?" At first glance, seeing both men side by side, one dressed as a highlander and the other a British officer, Iris imagined this was what the field might have looked like at Culloden before the fighting. Lieutenant Tytler's frown marred his face as Alex's playful one quirked a smile that made her giggle.

Alex released her hand as he spoke. "A character

from a play. William Shakespeare, in fact. Titania is queen of the fairies whose husband cast a spell on her, and Titania magically falls in love with a laborer. The laborer wears a donkey's head because he feels it's better suited for him."

Alex chuckled as he spoke. "After her husband had enough of watching Titania make a fool of herself to woo *a monster*, he reversed the spell, and the two reunited as Titania announced, *What visions have I seen! Methought I was enamored of an ass*." Alex used a high-pitched voice when quoting Titania's line, making him and Iris laugh.

Iris had to hold her stomach, she giggled so hard. "Oh, Mr. MacDougall, you do tease. That was quite good!" When they both stopped laughing, the officer stood there in awkward silence.

Iris adjusted her wig and smiled. "It's a satire, Lieutenant Tytler. A comedy full of whimsy."

Alex mumbled just loud enough for Iris to hear, "Something he is not familiar with."

The officer bowed. "Of course. You will save a dance for me later?" Iris stood still as he moved on.

Alex stood before her as his eyes traveled over her costume. "*A bhanrigh.*" *A queen.*

Iris felt playful, dressed as someone else. As though the character granted her the courage to be bold, she replied in Gaelic, *"Am bi thusa na mo rìgh?"* *Will you be my king?* She'd practiced the line repeatedly with Laurel and hoped she pronounced the words right.

Alex took her hand in his. "Titania not only had a king, Iris, but a husband. Oberon."

She stepped closer to him, a tilt in her grin. "That she did. But tonight, who will play the ass?" Alex burst into laughter, as did Iris.

Her father leaned over. "Alex, be a good man and take Iris for some refreshment. This damned greeting line will last the entire evening. Keep an eye on her for me, will you?"

Alex placed her hand on the crook of his arm. "My pleasure, Mi'Lord."

As they strolled away, Iris leaned close. "Thank you. That line was boring, and my feet hurt already." Alex led her to a chair, and she gratefully sat.

He bowed. "I shall return with refreshments."

Laurel came and sat beside her as John followed. Both wore highland clothing like Alex's. The plaids she recognized from the weekly Gael meetings. Alex's red with blue and green. John's shades of blue and Laurel's Comyn plaid was greener with a different pattern than Alex's.

Laurel laughed. "Oh, Iris. I've already danced the night away, and the evening's only begun."

John bowed before her. "Mi'Lady. Shall I get ye both a drink?"

Iris shook her head. "For Laurel, yes. Alex's gone to get me one already." John nodded and turned away.

Laurel took her hand. "So, ye already latched on to Alex?"

She grinned. "Yes. Father even tasked him to be my guard. Told him to keep an eye on me." Laurel raised an eyebrow.

Iris fingered her wig. "Lieutenant Tytler spoke to me in the greeting line. Said the wig made me look old."

Her friend barked a laugh. "That man could find fault anywhere." She patted her hand. "The wig is dramatic and very becoming on ye." Alex arrived and handed her a glass of punch. She took the offered refreshment, drinking it all.

Alex chuckled. "Thirsty, Iris?" He handed her his, and she drank that as well. John returned, and the four of them sat for a bit as Laurel and John whispered between themselves.

As the quartet took up a lively tune, Mr. Taft approached and offered his hand to Iris. "A dance with an old friend, Iris? The Mrs. isn't up to dancing, and I fancy a jig." Iris smiled and took his hand as she stood.

Alex stood bowing. "Return her here. I promised Lord Erskine I'd be her guardian."

Mr. Taft nodded and led her to the floor where other dancers skipped, twirling in a circle. They joined the dance, and soon, Iris spun around the floor. As she came around, Alex crossed to the refreshment table and picked up a glass, his focus never leaving her. Another circle around the room, her eyes connected with Lieutenant Tytler's, who watched her with a hooded gaze that left her uneasy.

The band soon stopped, and she held her stomach. "Oh, Mr. Taft, that was quite a dance. I shall have to sit." He escorted her back to Alex, who now sat with Laurel and John. Alex stood and offered her a glass of punch, which she gulped.

Mr. Taft bowed before her. "Thank you, Iris. A fine dancer as always."

The musicians started a slow waltz, and Alex took her glass, and handed the cup to John. "Here, John, look after that, will ye? I wish to waltz." He didn't ask but took Iris's hand and led her to the floor. If he had asked, she wouldn't have been able to reply. The look Alex settled on her as he took her into his arms nearly made her knees buckle.

With his hand on her waist, he pulled her close and whispered in her ear as he led her to the first step. "The waltz is the most beautiful of dances." Their bodies glided across the floor in perfect sync. The rise and fall of the strides with the melody were almost hypnotic.

She murmured back, "Is it the people dancing that is the beauty—or the people's movement itself?" Alex took her in a spin as he twirled them together with the crescendo of the music, then glided them along the side of the dancers in perfect timing with the music.

He stopped and stared at her momentarily, then took her into a gliding movement again. "The beauty of dance is the body communicates what words cannot."

He twirled them again and dipped her as he held her in his arms. "It is an expression of the time the dance came from."

He lifted her and spun them into a gliding movement down the room's length. "A waltz is a perfect blend of the abstract values and ideals of the Romantic era: freedom, character, passion, and expressiveness." As he spoke the last, he spun them again till they were so close their breaths mingled as they breathed. He stopped as the last notes of the violin resonated through the ballroom. They stayed close as the dancers clapped for the band. Iris couldn't move if she wanted. Alex moved away and bowed as he held her hand.

When Iris took her first step, she wobbled a little, and Alex held her beside him. "Do ye need some fresh air, Iris? Ye look a little flushed."

She nodded. "Fresh air, yes. The terrace is set with braziers to keep guests warm." She pointed to the twin doors leading to the balcony overlooking the gardens.

Alex took her hand in his arm and steered them to the door. Once through, he released her, and she went for the edge, taking in large breaths, thankful for the cooler temperatures. The snow hadn't fallen again and much of the ice had melted, but the chilly breeze helped clear her head.

He came up beside her. "Can I get ye anything, Iris?"

She turned. "Oh no. The dance was lovely. Thank you. You are a great dancer. I hadn't danced like that in a long time."

Alex nodded and moved closer. "My pleasure, Iris. Ye are a fine dancer as well." He smirked. "Not many can keep up with me. My ma taught me. I hold dear many of her traditions." He glanced around, and Iris hoped he'd spy what she'd placed outside.

When his eyes landed on the greenery hanging outside the door, his smile went wide. "Mistletoe hung for the New Year."

Iris giggled and dragged him to it. "A kiss under the mistletoe, for luck."

He followed but kept his distance. "Iris, I cannot kiss ye. I've reserved my kisses for someone else." Iris glanced down, keeping her face hidden despite wearing a mask. He kept his kisses for her, for Ivy. She wanted to tell him, but what would he say? And at the ball, would he make a scene? She didn't want to lose this moment but wanted to capture their time and hold the memory forever.

She glanced up at him. "One kiss for luck certainly won't make your friend upset. It's for the New Year."

Alex exhaled. "One for ye only, Iris." He bent close as their breaths blended.

As she closed her eyes, he brushed his lips over hers. She responded with gentle pressure. He deepened the kiss, and his tongue danced with hers as she gasped. Alex's arms came around her, and they kissed like they had before, like Ivy and Alex.

A loud throat clearing made her jump and Alex stepping back. His gaze met hers, and something crossed his expression, then disappeared. Had he recognized her?

Lieutenant Tytler's clipped voice sounded harsh in the evening air. "Iris, I believe you promised me a dance." She turned, and he stood by the other door. His expression was one of loathing. She shivered not from the cold breeze.

Alex bowed. "Mi'Lady." He strode past the officer and into the ballroom. Lieutenant Tytler's hand tapped his leg in a harsh rhythm as he glowered at her.

She grimaced and marched past him. "Your dance, Lieutenant."

She went to the dance floor and waited for the officer to follow. When he arrived, he took her harshly into his arms. The dance was a country group dance where they started as a pair, then broke apart in circles with other partners and came back in a line, where each pair skipped down the center.

They started the dance quickly enough, even though Lieutenant Tytler was rough handling her. When they broke apart, Iris heaved a sigh. Would the Lieutenant shove her around the ballroom the entire dance? When she followed the people in the circle, she spied Alex leaning against the wall by the doors to the terrace, watching her intently. John and Laurel were nowhere she'd seen. When they faced each other again for the line, Lieutenant Tytler's expression was stern.

They came together for their turn down the center of the pairs, and the officer hissed in her ear, "Care to join me outside, Iris?" As they neared the end of the people, she tried to pull away, but the Lieutenant had a firm hold of both her hands. When they reached the end of the line, he dragged her through the second set of open doors onto the terrace. He took her to the balcony edge and kissed her hard.

She reared back and slapped him. "You bastard."

He kissed her again and pulled back. "You'd kiss that filthy Scot and not an English officer." He grabbed her throat, squeezing hard.

She choked and tried to take in air, but his grip tightened as he yelled. "Are you a harlot now? Has the Scot dirtied the fine woman you are?" Stars danced before her eyes. From the sides, darkness crept into her vision. Her ears rang as she saw his mouth move, but she couldn't hear what he said. She pried at his hands and scratched as she tried to breathe.

Someone shoved them apart, and Iris fell to the ground, gasping in precious air. Her throat hurt something awful, but at least she breathed. When she glanced up, Alex punched Lieutenant Tytler, who rounded punching him as other guests gathered around them.

Her father forced his way through the crowd. "What is the meaning of this?"

Her mother followed, kneeling beside her. "Iris, darling, are you all right?"

Iris tried to speak, but nothing came out. Tears gathered in her eyes as pain radiated from her throat. Her hand went there, trying to smooth it.

Alex stood beside Lieutenant Tytler, panting. "He

choked her!"

The Lieutenant straightened his coat. "I did not." He pulled on his shirt cuffs, straightening them. "We kissed, and your colleague hit me in a jealous rage."

Iris cried out, but the sound came as a ragged whisper. "No!" When the itchy pain burned her throat, she coughed hard.

Her mother gathered her in her arms. "Something's happened. My baby has lost her voice." As her mother helped her rise, she stayed in her mother's arms, glad for what comfort she found there.

Lieutenant Tytler stood tall. "I demand justice." He turned to Alex, "Have your second meet with mine. Pistols at dawn."

Her father shoved between them. "Men, there is no need for something as illegal as dueling. And certainly not where I am Lord Justice over."

Laurel shoved her way through the crowd. "I saw it all. The English bloke dragged her here and forced himself on her. She slapped him." Many in the crowd gasped as Laurel continued, "He strangled her. I don't know what was said, but he was angry."

Lieutenant Tytler turned to Laurel. "How would you know? No one was out here."

Laurel grabbed John's arm. "We were in the shadows if ye'd bother to look around."

Her father bent to her. "Is it as Alex and Laurel say? Your voice is gone. Did Lieutenant Tytler attack you?"

Iris nodded as the reality of the moment settled in on her. The Lieutenant had attacked her. Hurt her for kissing Alex. Acting as if he believed he owned her. Tears gathered in her eyes.

Laurel stepped forward and took her hand. "Allow

me, Mi'Lady Erskine. I'll take her to her room. Get her some hot tea."

As Laurel led her away, her father's voice boomed. "Lieutenant Tytler, I suggest you leave before I press charges." Iris glanced back at the men, and the Lieutenant's eyes followed her. His expression held anger and promised revenge for the slight delivered to him so publicly. Her eyes traveled to Alex, and his eyes crinkled as his gaze followed her. What started as a joyous evening ended in something unexpected. Iris had gotten her kiss from Alex under the mistletoe, but at what price?

****

The following day, Iris spent most of her time in her bedroom. She sat beside the window as the sun passed slowly over her. It hadn't snowed, but the cold filtered through the window, chilling her. Her bedroom faced the garden, and she wished for spring and the greenery's return.

Laurel came in with a tray of tea and cakes. "Another cup of tea, Iris?"

Iris shook her head and spoke, but her voice came out raspy. She coughed and then mouthed. *If I drink another cup of tea, I might float away.* Her mouth formed the last part, and she made her hands like a boat on the water. Laurel set the tray on the table beside her, smiled, and sat beside her.

First thing this morning, the doctor came to see her and declared her voice strained from the Lieutenant's attack. She was on orders not to speak, but with Laurel, she tried out of sheer frustration.

Iris sighed as she stared at the bare garden, amazed at the irony of the situation she had found herself in. Ivy, who couldn't speak, was now Iris, who'd lost her voice. Laurel's warning echoed, *The fly flying into the spider's web*. What a web she'd woven.

"Iris, I've come to check on you, dear." Her father's voice had her turning in her chair. Iris stood at her father's entry.

He leaned against the doorway as he glanced between her and Laurel. "Lieutenant Tytler came first thing this morning." He exhaled. "I sent him away. I hope that was your desire, daughter." Iris nodded, not wanting to speak in front of her father. Not from the doctor's orders, but after last night, she honestly didn't know what to say.

"Alex MacDougall just left. He asked after your welfare. He said he wished you well and hopes you recover fully."

His gaze moved to Laurel as he held up a letter. "Alex sent you another note, Laurel."

As Laurel stepped forward to take the parchment, he flipped the letter up, and his eyes moved to Iris. "But I suspect it's for you, Iris. Isn't it?"

Her maid gasped and turned to Iris. "Mi'Lady?" Iris stood taller as she waved Laurel away.

As Laurel passed her father, he stopped her with his hand. "Laurel, you care for Iris well. I thank you for that." She nodded and moved past him out of the room.

He crossed to her and handed her the note. "Ivy? An interesting nickname, daughter."

She took the parchment and stared at the curvy writing on the front. Alex had written *Ivy* in a scrolling script and drawn ivy vines around it. She flipped the letter over, and his familiar red wax seal of *M* with vines held the document closed. Her fingers brushed the seal.

When her father cleared his throat, she turned and set his message on the tray, unopened.

She turned back to her father, who watched her with a keen eye. "Alex, you are fond of him?" Iris stammered and tried whispering, but the sound came out too raspy as speaking hurt her throat.

She twirled and sat hard in her chair, placing her head in her hands, then glanced up at him as if to beg for help.

He sat in the chair opposite her and patted her hands. "The letters from Alex. They were all for you, weren't they?" She tried to pull her hands from his, but he wouldn't let go. She sighed and nodded.

He returned her nod. "I knew Alex had a new pursuit. But when I saw you with him at the Tea Room those weeks ago, I wondered what you were up to."

Iris began to speak, but her father held up a hand. "Don't strain your voice. I don't know if I want to know what game you play." He lowered his hand with a sigh. "I'll keep your mother out of it. What I want you to know is Alex is a very honorable man. He's well-educated and bright. I admire him as a fellow solicitor and as my friend." Iris sat up and waved her hand in a circle, encouraging him to continue.

Her father exhaled. "You want to know more?" He chuckled, releasing her hand, and sat back in the chair. "He's worked through his studies during the hardest time this country has seen and survived. He's taken on a tough position straddled between the culture he loves and his duty as a servant to the English crown. As a matter of fact, he begged for his position, saying this was his destiny to serve. Said that he needed to make amends with Scotland." Iris smiled as she glanced out the window. She knew Alex took his work seriously, and the Gaels followed him without question.

Her father's voice brought her focus back to him. "He's the first son of Laird Roderick and Lady Mary MacDougall. He will retain the lairdship upon his father's death. His family owns two castles that his father managed to keep ownership of during the clearances in a bargain with the Campbells over his whisky trade. A wise move that's saved his ancestral homes."

He stared out the window. "Their family is sometimes called cowards since his father refused to bring the clan to fight at Culloden." How awful. What she knew of Alex, coward was the last word she'd use to describe him.

His voice brought her back to the conversation. "His father claimed his wife burned his feet, and he couldn't lead them." Her father chuckled as he glanced back at her. "I suspect he knew what the Scottish were up against. Wise man if you ask me. Risked his reputation to save hundreds of clansmen's lives." Tears gathered in her eyes at the thought of constantly being called a coward for the actions of your sire. Alex was much like her father. Both held an unwavering devotion to family and justice.

He reached over and squeezed her hand. "Alex is no coward, but a hard worker, a fighter." He let go of her hand and stood as he straightened his coat. "Any man would be honored to call him friend." He crossed to the door. Alex had so many great qualities. Iris smiled as a tear fell.

She wiped the droplet away before her father stopped and turned at the door. "Get well, Iris. And make sure you read your letter from your sweetheart."

As he left her, her focus turned to the tray, and the note glowed in the afternoon sunlight. With the sun and the shadow, the raised seal looked almost like a heart. Iris grabbed the letter from the tray and held his message to her heart. What would Alex say?

She slid her finger under the seal, and the paper tore a little when she opened the fold. Iris held the paper in the sunlight.

Dearest Ivy,

I miss you so. Please ride with me this afternoon, 2 pm—the College Garden entrance gates. I hope you can get away. I am counting the seconds till I hold you in my arms again.

Yours truly,

Alex

The wall clock downstairs chimed once. Iris gasped, one in the afternoon. Damn, that gave her little time to change as she needed forty minutes at minimum to ride across town. What would Alex do if she were late? She crossed the room and stuck her head out the door, attempting to call out, but her voice came as a weak breath that hurt her throat.

Laurel appeared from the room next door. "Yer father's gone already?" She came to her. "Is our game exposed? Do I still have a job?" Iris took her hands in hers and shook her head.

She mouthed the words as she pulled Laurel into the room. *My father knows but keeps our secret. Hurry. I'm to meet Alex.* Iris turned and dug in her armoire, then held up her riding outfit.

Laurel folded her arms. "It would be so much easier if ye just told Alex who ye really are."

Chapter 12

Mac stopped the cart a short way from the College Garden entry gates. "Sorry Pixie turned up lame, Mi'Lady. Are ye sure ye want me to drop ye here?" He glanced around. "Why 'tis no one about. The lord would be right angry if anything happened to ye."

Iris jumped down from the wagon seat and moved around the team of horses till she came beside Mac and shook her head. She adjusted her borrowed cloak, ensuring the slight bruising on her neck from the prior evening stayed covered as she marched to the gate. She'd left her hair loose and a portion blew into her face, as the strands captured the sunlight, and the auburn tones stood out more—the hair color Alex associated with Ivy.

Mac called out. "Well, if ye need me to pick ye up, send word." Iris turned and waved, then bundled herself tighter. When she turned the corner of the gates and moved into the gardens, Alex sat mounted on Oberon. As her boots crunched the grass, he turned, and when his eyes met hers, he smiled wide.

When she neared, he glanced around. "Ivy, where's yer mount?" Iris limped the last few steps, prancing like a horse.

Alex dismounted and took her hands. "Yer horse came up lame?" She nodded. Alex lifted her onto his horse. She yelped, but the sound came out as air. Before she could adjust her seat, Alex swung up behind her and gathered her in his arms, pulling her close to him.

His breath brushed her ear. "No matter. I wanted an excuse to get ye into my arms, and now I have it." Holding her tight, he kneed Oberon in a trot and went around the gardens at a clipped pace. His horse skipped and pulled on the reins. Alex kept a hold of him while keeping her in his arms. She leaned back into him, and his warmth spread across her back. He hummed as she shifted and turned a little so she rested her head against his chest.

He stopped his horse and stared down into her face. "Oberon wants a run. I planned to ride out to the country a pace, then double back." He kissed her full on the mouth. "Ready for a run?" Iris nodded, and Alex adjusted her before him. He made a clicking noise and kneed Oberon, who reared a little and took off at a run. Alex's arms tightened on her as he leaned forward, molding his body against her.

Oberon cleared the end of the cobble streets onto the dirt road, stretching his head as he took them past pastures filled with sheep and then fields. Soon, all she saw was the vast open country with knolls rolling over hills. Alex slowed Oberon to a trot, then a walk, and the horse blew his breath.

Alex chuckled as he patted Oberon's neck. "Needed that, did ye, boy?" Oberon tossed his head as they continued at a walk. The silence stretched, and Iris was content with the quiet as she took in the countryside. With all that had happened, she needed to get away from the city, from herself.

Humming softly, he leaned in and whispered in her ear, "I missed ye at the ball." Iris tried to turn, but she only caught his profile.

His mouth shifted to a firm line. "It is good ye were not there. I am certain yer cousin filled ye in." He blew his breath. "That damned Lieutenant Tytler. He's got it out for the Scots and takes his duty too seriously, ensuring there are no Jacobites left. It's left the Scottish people fearful of him." Iris stiffened at the mention of the Lieutenant. Curious to what Alex thought of the whole situation, being Ivy, she was open to asking more about it. She nodded as her hand moved to her throat, and her eyes met his.

He growled. "Aye, I figured Laurel told ye what he did to poor Iris. Being Lord Erskine's daughter, ye'd think the damned fool would know not to try to have his way with her."

He stopped Oberon. "I have a confession to make." He brushed his hand on her cheek. "I kissed another, but the gesture was a friendly kiss. One for luck, for Iris. I felt she needed it." Iris tried to whisper, but with the colder air in the country, her throat tightened, and she began coughing.

Alex patted her back. "Is the cold getting to ye?" She wanted to tell him, to explain that she was Iris. She wanted to say thank you for saving her from the Lieutenant. But now that she was ready, her throat wouldn't allow it. She huffed. She wanted to shout, yes, she needed his kiss last night and most of all now. She pointed to her and then him and tried to speak again, but a squeak came out.

Alex took her hand in his and kissed it. "Ivy, it's all right. I understand. Ye are trying to say it's okay that I helped Iris."

She shook her head, pointed to her, and threw her hood off, but Alex pulled the covering back on. "Ivy, I know ye say it's okay. I will always help those in need, and I thank ye for understanding." He kissed her, and she kissed him back, hoping all her emotions shared what her voice couldn't. Alex shifted and thrust his tongue in, and Iris relished the taste of him, of them. With his movement in the saddle, Oberon sidestepped and skipped, but Alex flexed his legs, keeping the animal under control.

Alex lifted his head. "I guess Oberon still needs a run." He shifted her and took the reins. "Let's let him have his race back to the city. I have something planned for this afternoon." They rode back to the city at a full gallop. Iris sat back into Alex's arms, thankful for his comfort and security. When they entered the city's outskirts, Alex turned. They rode beside Glasgow Cathedral, across the burn, then up the hill. At the crest, Alex stopped Oberon, who stamped once and then settled.

From the rise, stretched out before them, lay all of Glasgow. At this vantage point, Iris saw from one end of the city to the other onto the banks of the Clyde River. The streets held people and horses that moved about but looked so little, like her childhood doll house.

She breathed a sigh as Alex whispered in her ear. "Magnificent, isn't it?" He dismounted and held his arms up to her. She slid easily into his arms as he bent and kissed her. Alex then turned and untied the saddle bag, removed wrapped items, and handed them to her individually. He strode to the other side and pulled a wine bottle and tartan from the saddle bag.

When he came beside her, he kissed her cheek. "Come, Ivy, let me show ye my favorite place in the city." He moved to the hill's edge before a tree, spread the tartan on the ground, and then set the wine on a corner. Iris followed and tapped his arm, then pointed to Oberon.

Alex grinned as he took the items from her arms. "He's a trained warhorse. He won't wander." With his arms empty, he took her in and kissed her. His lips, tongue, and body consumed her senses at once. When he lifted his head, she became a little dizzy. Alex rotated her until she stood before him and lowered them to the ground. He settled her in his arms and between his legs as he sat back against the tree. She warmed with his cloak and hers, and he moved, wrapping them in a cocoon. As Alex grabbed the wine bottle, he uncorked the wine and then took a pull. He handed the vessel to her. She eyed him, then took a healthy sip.

He unwrapped each item, sliced beef, cheese, and bread. His offering was a simple meal but perfect for outdoors. Alex held the meat. Iris reached out to take the beef, but he shook his head, insisting he feed her. They continued in silence, her one bite for his two to three. Soon, they settled back against the tree, nestled in each other's arms.

Alex hummed. "I used to come up here a lot when I attended college. I dreamt of all the great things I'd do with an education. Dreamt of the grand future of Scotland and how I'd shape it." He chuckled. "Big dreams they were. Up here, I felt like Oberon, King of the Fae." He took another swig. "I wondered at what my future would hold." Iris turned in his arms, and he handed her the wine. She held the bottle but tried to speak. Her voice came out as a squeak again.

She took a sip and tried whispering. "You…" but the cold air had her coughing again.

Alex held her and helped her drink more. "Ivy, don't hurt yerself speaking." She handed him the wine and sat up shifting out of his arms. She pointed to him and then made the King's crown like she had when she asked about him being the leader of the Gaels. She pounded her fist to her chest and nodded as Alex set the bottle down.

Alex took her in his arms. "Oh, Ivy. I know ye try to tell me what I've done is good but is it enough? Will the Scottish culture survive the English King's rule?" He grumbled. "Can we all truly live together in peace?" She sat up and nodded as the breeze shifted her hair blowing the whisps against her cheeks.

He brushed the hair off her face. "Ye believe we will, don't ye?" She nodded again and kissed him. He returned the kiss and moved her till she fell under him. They kissed until wet drops hit Iris' face. Alex lifted his head as Iris opened her eyes—snow fell, hitting her face.

Alex pulled her up. "Sorry, lass. I didn't notice the clouds." He quickly packed up their meal placing the wrapping in the saddle bag.

When he came back, he took her hands. "My da would have my hide if he knew I'd been so careless." He lifted her to the saddle. "Guess I've been away from the country too long to note simple snow clouds."

He mounted behind her and cued Oberon into a smooth gallop. "Let's get inside before we get covered in snow."

****

After stabling Oberon, Alex led her through the back much as he had the day after Christmas, but this time, the kitchens were spotless. He took her through the hall and into the parlor. Along the way, he shed his cloak and dumped the garment on a settee in the hall. He strode to the fireplace in the parlor and bent to start a fire. Iris went to him and tapped his shoulder.

He rose and took her hands in his. "I'll have a fire lit soon to get ye warm." She shook her head and pulled his hands as she backed toward the door. She didn't want to be in the parlor. She wanted to be in his bedroom, in his bed.

As she backed up, a grin spread across his face. "Ye don't want to be in here, do ye, Ivy?" She twisted and held one hand as she led him up the stairway. As she turned at the top, Alex's light chuckle followed her as they moved down the hallway to his room.

John poked his head out of his door. "Ah, checking to see if Alex made it home. Good to see ye, Ivy." He nodded to Alex. "Laurel said we must be up early to get the ladies back to the manor before the missus finds out they've been out all night."

Alex nodded as Iris pulled his hand. She wanted Alex to herself and didn't want any more delays. When she pushed open the door, the fire burned low—the only light in the dim room. Alex passed her and placed a log on the fire. Iris removed her cloak and laid the coat on the chair. When she turned around, Alex stood before her.

He took her into his arms and held her for a moment. "I relish having ye in my arms, Ivy." He bent and kissed her neck, then her ear. She gasped as his tongue trailed to her lips, where he kissed her softly. Alex lifted his head as his eyes traveled over her face. His hand rose and brushed her cheek then lowered to her neck fingering the marks there.

His gaze rose to hers. "Accident?" Iris's hand went there, covering the mark as she pulled back. Firm arms brought her back into his embrace. "Ah, Ivy, ye don't need to hide a burn or yer hard work." He bent kissing the mark. Iris thought about telling him about her then and there but his fingers trailed a path from her cheek to her neck and to her breast. He tilted his head as the back of his hand moved back and forth over her breasts, making her breath come faster chasing all rational thought away.

Alex bent and brushed a kiss on her neck as he turned her in his arms. At her back, his hands made quick work of her stays, untying them till her bodice loosened, and he pulled the garment away. Freed from the pressure, Iris took a deep breath and turned toward him. Alex untied her shift as she ran her hands under his coat over his chest. As he bent and kissed her bare shoulder, she caressed his till his coat slid off. His lips came back to hers in a passionate kiss.

He quickly spun her and untied her skirt. "Ye wear entirely too many clothes for my desires." The fabric soon fell to the floor, and her shift came over her head in a billowy wave. His body came flush with hers as he kissed her neck and trailed kisses down her back. His hands untied her garters and rolled down one hose, then the other. He tickled her ankle bringing out a gasp as she lifted her foot and he removed her shoe, then her stocking, leaving her clothes on the floor.

He took her hand as he rose and led her to the bed. When he pushed her down, she stood firm and shook her head. She untied his cravat and pulled the material from his neck. His hands rose to remove his shirt, and she batted them away, preferring to disrobe him as he had her.

Alex raised an eyebrow. "The lady desires to

undress me? Yer wish is my command." He stood with his hands by his side as Iris ran her hands under and over his naked chest as the springy hair ruffled her fingers.

As with his coat, she pushed the garment over his shoulders then glided the material down his arms until he was free. Her hands brushed the front of his trousers, and he sucked in a breath. She untied the ties and unlaced them as she smiled at him. He chuckled and kicked his boots off, then bent and pulled his pants free in one motion. His socks came off, and he stood as bare as her.

As his hand landed on her shoulder, his head bent and brushed a kiss on her lips as her hands returned to his chest. She loved the feel of his hair tickling her fingertips as she explored, her palms molding his muscles. His kiss turned urgent, making her rise on her toes to take in more of his caress and more of him.

Alex lifted his head and grinned at her as he pushed her until she lay on the bed. He leaned over her, kissing her lips and then her neck. As he shifted back, he kissed her breast, suckling a nipple. She arched into his fondling and reached for him.

His head lifted as a devilish expression crossed his face. As he moved farther down her body, he kissed her navel, then her stomach. Iris arched again and closed her eyes, reveling in his attentions. She sensed he shifted, and warm air blew on her curls. He moved her knees apart, allowing them to rest on the edge of the bed.

His breath blew again, tickling her, and his tongue licked her there. She sat up, but his hand on her stomach stopped her. She glanced down, and he licked her again as his eyes settled on her.

His fingers touched, spreading her. His mouth closed over her, and waves shot through her body. She arched and cried out, but her voice came as a whisper. He suckled her, and the pressure she'd felt with him before building again. As he moved his mouth on her, his tongue swirled, hitting a point that sent another shock wave through her body. Her legs came up, and his hand rested on one knee, holding her in place.

When he lifted his head, his fingers rubbed the area, sending waves of pleasure through her. She shook her head as he played her like a fine instrument, making music between them. Alex bent and sucked her again as he inserted a finger. She arched as she lifted her hips, meeting each thrust.

As his hand moved, he shifted over her and kissed her hard. "Ivy, ye drive me crazy. I must have ye." He pulled her hips to the end of the bed and positioned him at her entrance.

He rubbed himself over her, spreading the moisture. "Ivy, open yer eyes. I wish to see the pleasure I bring ye." She gave into his request and gazed into him as he entered her, slowly filling her. When he fully seated himself, he threw his head back in a sigh and began moving within her. First, slowly, with his head back, he held her hips as if his motions caressed her. He bent his head to watch their joining and picked up the pace, driving into her fully with each thrust.

As her body flashed hot, then cold, the pressure returned in full force. She writhed as each stroke drove her closer to the edge. Closer to that burst of pleasure she'd found in his arms. His fingers dug into her hips as his thrust drove into her repeatedly. Unable to contain herself anymore, the damn burst, and she cried out in a hoarse whisper. In two more thrusts, Alex followed her to heaven. He roared her name as he froze, holding her tightly.

Alex pumped once, then again, and slowly, her body released him. He fell into the bed beside her and pulled her into his arms. "Ivy, lord. What ye do to me." She tried to sit up but couldn't. Alex chuckled, sat up to his knees, and slipped from the bed. Picking her up, he threw the covers back and slid her into the bed with him, holding her in his arms as he pulled the covers over them.

They lay naked in each other's arms as her breaths slowed and her heart calmed. The echoes of their loving sent shivers through her body, and Alex squeezed her once. She rested her head on his chest as her fingers moved over it. His breathing slowed, and his heartbeat lulled her to sleep, cradled in his embrace.

****

Dawn came too fast. A block from the manor, she tapped him, signaling he needed to stop Oberon. He dismounted and held his arms out to her. She slid into his arms and hugged him quickly. The sun was already up. She needed to hurry.

She turned away, and he grabbed her hand, pulling her to him as he held her tightly. "I love ye, Ivy." Her breath caught. She lifted her head as a tear escaped. How she wished he'd said *Iris* that he knew who she was and loved *her*. She blew her breath as another tear fell.

He caught it. "Please don't cry, Ivy. Just show me yer heart." Another tear fell, and she took his hand and placed his palm over her heart. Her eyes connected with his, and she nodded as if to say, *and I you.*

Alex smiled. "I, as well, Ivy. Till next week at the Gaels meeting." He strode away, followed by John, who'd said his goodbyes to Laurel. John mounted and took off at a trot into the morning light. Alex mounted

Oberon and turned the animal around. He nodded to her, then kneed his horse into a gallop as he rode into the morning sun. Iris's knees gave way. If Laurel hadn't caught her, she'd have been a heap on the ground.

Laurel's breath blew in her ear. "He loves ye. He said he loves ye." God, she loved him back with all her heart.

Iris's tear-stained face rose to her friends as she whispered in broken sounds, "He loves Ivy, not Iris. What will I do now?"

****

As both men rode past, a cloaked figure sat atop his horse, hidden in the shadows. Snow dusted his shoulders, and the wind blew his already frozen form. But the discomfort was worth it. To stay out all night waiting for this moment—to witness her betrayal. Lieutenant Tytler's mood lifted, as he spied Iris's stupid maid leading her to the manor house. That whore, she had no idea whom she dealt with. His scrutiny moved to the retreating form of Alex MacDougall and his companion. That bastard Jacobite will get everything that's coming to him and more. He'll hang for sure, and then Iris will fall into his arms. This was right. With the sunrise, he felt God blessed his actions.

Chapter 13

Alex stood on a wooden box as he spoke to his friends at the Gaels meeting. "Scotsmen, Scotswomen. It's our duty to keep the Scottish culture alive. The King may rule, but is that sacrifice really worth yer livelihood, yer very lives?" Murmurs moved through the crowd, and his eyes roamed the people there. Mabina beamed at him. Others nodded as their expressions held firm. When he lifted his eyes to the back of the crowd, Ivy stood beside Laurel as his love stared at him.

He stood taller as he spoke from his heart. "We must live on. Carry Scotland in our hearts and soul. So we will live to see another day!" As his gaze held Ivy's, the crowd erupted into cheers. He stepped down from the box and made his way through the gathering to her. He got stopped a few times as he progressed toward Ivy, but his eyes never left hers. She'd been busy at the manor and had only been to one meeting this month. This one was well attended, and the energy was palpable in the crowd.

When he finally reached her, he took her in his arms and spun her in a circle. "Ivy, I am so glad to see ye." He bent and kissed her full on the mouth. She responded, and her smile went wide when he lifted his head.

He took her hand and pulled her into the mass of people. "Ivy, there's people I want ye to meet. Friends of mine." A shrill whistle blew loudly as soldiers on horseback flooded the area under the bridge. Men wearing the king's colors yelled as they guided their horses into the crowd. Men hollered, and women screamed. Alex grabbed Ivy's hand and pulled her to the side of the mass.

A familiar English voice shouted over the commotion. "Arrest them all. I want every one of them taken into custody." Alex jolted at Lieutenant Tytler's voice as he searched the crowd. His focus stopped finding the lieutenant's easily enough.

The British officer pointed to Alex. "Him, that's their leader. Alex MacDougall. Take him now!" Red coats swarmed him, pulling him from Ivy. A fist punched his face, another his stomach.

Lieutenant Tytler's voice came again. "Guard the exits. I want no criminals escaping."

Alex turned and caught Ivy in the arms of a soldier as she struggled to break free. "Ivy!"

Her head lifted as the red coat placed cuffs on his hands, securing them behind his back. Lieutenant Tytler sauntered to him as two other officers held him. Ivy stood frozen, her eyes wide as she stared at him.

The British officer punched his face forcing Alex's head to the side. He hit his stomach once, then again and again. A woman's voice called out over the crowd. Its English accent was clear and stark at night. His head lifted, and his eyes met Ivy's. Tears streamed down her face.

He called out to her again. "Ivy!"

The lieutenant turned and followed his gaze. Ivy called out, but the voice didn't fit a Scotswoman.

It came out loud, clear, and crisp in an English accent. "Alex, no!"

Glancing between the two, the officer spoke, "Ivy? You mean Iris. You address Lady Iris Erskine, Lord Erskine's daughter." Ivy broke free of the soldiers and ran to Alex.

She gripped his coat. "Alex, please…" Her clipped English accent rang hard in his ears as his heart plummeted to his toes. She'd lied this whole time. Allowed him to believe she was Scots when, all along, she was—one of them.

Lieutenant Tytler broke into a laugh so menacing the sound chilled him to his bones. "Oh, this is grand. I couldn't have planned this better if I tried." He nodded to the soldier behind Ivy, no Iris, who took her arms and held them behind her.

The lieutenant addressed the soldier. "Arrest her. She is with the traitors."

Iris struggled in the hold. "I am not a traitor. These people are not traitors! They only seek to be true to their culture. No one argues the King's rule." Her voice grated on Alex's ears. Of all the sounds he imagined she'd emit, this was the last he thought he'd ever hear from her sweet lips.

The officer turned away from her and locked gazes with Alex. "Take the whore away. I will deal with her later after I speak with her lover, the leader of the Jacobites." They scuffled, and her cry echoed. Alex lowered his gaze refusing to look at her. He couldn't after her disloyalty.

Lieutenant Tytler's low chuckle came to him as he stared at the ground—mocking and brittle. "You didn't know. All this time, you courted her." He stepped forward, his face coming beside Alex's as he jeered. "You fucked her. Sullied the fine woman she was." He huffed, "And you didn't know she was English." Her betrayal burned in his soul. How could she?

As Alex lifted his head, glaring at Lieutenant Tytler, he pulled back, *"Fuck dheth!" Fuck off.*

At the Lieutenant's confused expression, Alex's anger rose. *"Tha thu nad rud sam bith agus bidh thu gu bràth." You are nothing and will forever be nothing.*

He stood tall and stared down at the Lieutenant. *"Tha mi gad mhallachadh gu ifrinn agus cha bhi smachd agad gu bràth ort no." I curse you to hell and will never be controlled by you or anyone.* A sharp pain exploded in the back of Alex's head. Lieutenant Tytler's face swam before him as blackness closed in.

****

Iris stood and paced the length of the cell again. The women overcrowded the room, what room there was, but she couldn't just sit there.

She turned to Laurel. "It can't be that long before my father comes."

Laurel opened her mouth to reply, but another woman spoke. "Ye!"

She stood and pointed at Iris from the other side of the room. "It was ye that brought the English upon our secret meetings."

Her accuser sidestepped one woman on the floor and moved to Iris as the other women in the cell shifted away. "I heard yer voice. English as can be."

When she arrived at Iris, she turned, facing the others. "Told us all she was Ivy and couldn't speak." She turned back, sneering at Iris. "Lied to us all to spy for that Lieutenant." Her accuser spat at her feet.

Iris moved forward. "It's not that way. I promise." She waved her hands to the side. "I love Scottish people and your culture."

The Scots woman stood taller as Iris continued, *"Dh' ionnsaich eadhon Gàidhlig airson bruidhinn rithe." Even learned Gaelic to speak with you.* The woman turned, giving Iris her back.

Lieutenant Tytler approached the cell door. He waved to the guard who unlocked it. When the door swung open, the women gasped as they moved to the far side of the cell, huddling together. Laurel pulled Iris with her.

Lieutenant Tytler moved into the cell with two other guards flanking him. "Already breaking another law, Iris. Speaking their gutter language." He waved the two officers to her. They moved forward, grabbing her arms and pulling her toward the Lieutenant. Laurel held on to her, but they pulled her away.

Mabina grabbed Laurel. "Best ye stay out of it." As Iris struggled hard, the men dragged her to Lieutenant Tytler.

When she stood before the lieutenant, he gripped her face squeezing hard. "You had to ruin everything, didn't you?" As he held her face in a tight grip, forcing her mouth open, he kissed her. "You should have chosen more wisely, Iris, then you wouldn't need punishment."

His hand came away and slapped her hard. The blow forced her head to the side, and the impact burned her face. Her ears rang as she hung her head. The sound of a knife cutting her stays drifted to her, and her bodice loosened. She struggled against the men holding her, but her efforts only made her top fall farther. Another slap hit her head. Women called out, but they came from far-off.

The Lieutenant ripped her bodice from her body.

When her head came up, he held a large knife before her face. His grin went wide as he slid the blade into her shift and cut the garment down the middle, exposing her naked chest. She pulled on her arms to cover them, but the men held her hard as they chuckled.

Mabina's voice came from far away. "No, Laurel. They'll hurt ye too."

Iris struggled violently, and Lieutenant Tytler stepped back. "Careful, dear, you don't want to get cut." He twirled the blade as he gazed at it. "Well, not until I am ready to deliver full punishment." He hit her face again, the blow burning.

Lieutenant Tytler's eyes returned to the men holding her, and he nodded to his right. "Lay her down over there."

They dragged her to the side, and one man kicked her ankles as her feet flew out from under her as her back hit the floor hard. They knelt on either side of her, holding her arms as she lay on the ground. Women's screams filled the chamber as Iris's blood pumped in her ears. Her mind couldn't register all before her. The moment all seemed like a nightmare played in her head, yet this was real.

Lieutenant Tytler stepped to her feet. He sneered as he unbuttoned and removed his jacket, passing his knife hand to hand as his eyes roamed her body. Under his glare, she felt dirty and struggled anew, fearing what would come next.

He twirled the knife and threw the dagger at her. She yelped flinching as the blade landed beside her right hip. When her focus returned to him, he unbuttoned his trews and knelt as he pulled open her legs.

Women's screams filled the air as Lieutenant Tytler

moved closer. Iris closed her eyes, and when his hand touched her bare inner thigh, she screamed as loud as she could.

Sounds came in a jumble and yells filled her head. The Lieutenant moved away, and the men holding her let go. Finally freed, Iris curled into a ball, crying as she shrieked again. Held firmly one moment, released the next, Iris curled in, waiting for the first moment of pain as screams filled the air.

Arms encircled her. She jolted till her father's voice whispered in her ear, "Baby, I am here. Iris, you are safe." He rocked her. She cried harder as he took her in his lap.

His stern voice echoed in her ear, but the words brought comfort. "Arrest Lieutenant Tytler for assault and attempted rape." He shook a little. "The two officers with him and the guard as well."

Her father set her aside and stood, pulling his coat off and bent, wrapping the garment around her. He swept her in his arms, and she turned her head into the comfort of his embrace. Embarrassed beyond belief, Iris didn't want to see anyone and wished no one saw her.

They moved a little, and he stopped. "The women. Free them." The women's gasps came to her, but she kept her eyes closed, wishing to be anywhere but here.

Laurel's voice came close. "Let's get her home, Mi'Lord."

He took a deep breath. "Yes, home."

****

Alex sat in his cell, one separate from the others—a criminal left alone with a guard. It'd been two weeks since his arrest. Lord Erskine sent a colleague twice to explain the case against him and the actions taken on his behalf. As Lord Judge, Lord Erskine couldn't visit him personally. But the man he'd sent for Alex's defense, George Hamilton, Alex knew well. They'd given him a change of clothes, toiletries, and water. Food was plentiful, and a brazier warmed his cell, likely due to outrageous bribes from Lord Erskine. Legally and physically, he was in good hands—his heart however was another matter.

George stood before him outside the bars. "Sir, the trial begins soon. Due to your position, Lord Erskine cannot judge the case. So, they will be sending a judge from Edinburgh. He's due to arrive any day. Lord Erskine feels you have a good, solid defense." They'd discussed this before but George seemed to need to repeat it.

Paper rustled as he flipped the pages he held. "John's case was today. Lord Erskine released him with a fine. The other men as well." He looked up and sighed. "Only your case is left, being the accused leader."

Alex nodded as he stood before George. The bars came into view as the man behind them dimmed, looking like the prisoner. Yet Alex was on the inside. George put his papers in his case and set the satchel on the floor.

He stood and cleared his throat as he adjusted his coat. "Lord Erskine begged me to inform you…"

His weight shifted from foot to foot. "He asked if you've asked about her, about Iris."

Alex closed his eyes and bowed his head. God, it hurt to think of her. Even more so as her image flashed in his mind, in his memory. His throat closed as his eyes watered.

As Alex cleared his throat, his voice came out gruff. "The guard informed me Lord Erskine released the women."

His colleague shuffled his feet. "But Iris…"

Shouting, Alex cut him off. "Don't speak her name, *ever* in my presence!"

George replied, "But Alex…"

Alex yelled as loud as he could. "I don't want to know!"

He turned away, leaned against the bars, and crumpled as he slid down to sit on the dirt floor. "Leave me."

The sound of papers rustling came to him. There was a shuffle of feet and the guard bidding George goodbye. The slam of the outer iron door closing told Alex George had thankfully followed his order. He sat there with his eyes closed, trying not to picture Iris, but her image came to him anyway. Her smile and her silly hand motions to communicate. The feeling of her kisses. Her sweet expressions as he made love to her. Next came an image that was seared into his brain forever and eternity. Iris's face when she screamed his name in her English accent. Her tears, her expression. He hit the floor willing the nightmare all away.

Soft footfalls roused him. He must have dozed off. Alex sat there wondering who would come to see him, the criminal leader of the Glasgow Jacobites. He didn't bother turning and figured the sound might have only been the guard moving about. He settled back and closed his eyes. A moment passed, and then there was a light sigh and silence.

"I came as soon as I could." The sweet female's voice came to him, its British accent grating. Iris. He stiffened—her voice was so *English*. He tried to block her from his mind, but he couldn't. Her feet shuffled again. Her scent came to him, light with musky floral. Something that was uniquely her. He blew hard, ignoring its draw.

A small, wrapped napkin appeared next to him.

He caught a glimpse of her slender fingers as she let go of the package. "I brought you some sweet rolls." The scent of freshly baked bread wafted toward him, the yeasty, toasted aroma mingling with a hint of sweetened butter, making his stomach rumble.

Alex sensed her move away as she spoke, "The guard checked my packet for a weapon." She chuckled. "He stole one, claiming payment for allowing in a forbidden item." He hardened himself against her charms. Her innocence, an act—her betrayal still burned deeply. Had she lured the Lieutenant to the Gaels as others claimed? Her sole purpose—to infiltrate and oust them to the English officers. Or was she truly, as she claimed, an English lass interested in the mysterious and dangerous Scots?

Before the officers separated him from the other prisoners, many claimed the former—that she was a spy. George seemed to hint at something else. She sniffled and hiccupped a sigh. Now, the tears. She was a good actress—had fooled all of them.

"Alex, please."

He shook his head, not daring to voice an answer, fearing he'd give in to his desires for her.

Her dress shifted, and she puffed a sob as her voice came out shaky. "Alex, please forgive me. I am so, so sorry." The last came out a whisper. Had he paid attention earlier, he'd have seen the English mannerisms in her. But he was too blinded by her beauty. By her—to notice.

He sat there, not daring to move.

She stood still, frozen as well.

The silence stretched between them.

The sunlight shifted again, and the room's energy changed.

Alex sensed her shift.

Something different came over her. "I'll prove myself to you. I don't know how, but some way, I'll prove my love and devotion, Alex."

He barked at her. "Never allow my name to spill from yer lips. Yer accent, I cannot stand, and yer betrayal I cannot abide. Never seek me again." When he blurted the last, he turned his head, and the edge of her skirt, her light blue cloak over it, waved. She sobbed, and the skirt fluttered as her footsteps made quick beats at her exit. The slam of the iron gate confirmed she'd fled.

Good, gone from his life. He could focus on what was important—proving his innocence while retaining his job. He owed this to Scotland to make amends for the travesties his mistake caused. The silence filled him. He took comfort in the emptiness as he watched the dust flutter in the sunbeams shining through the window's prison bars. The light leaving the striped pattern over his legs reminded him that he was a prisoner of the very crown he had sworn an oath to and served.

The iron gate squeaked with its swing. The sound familiar to him announcing another guest. It wasn't mealtime, and the guard kept to himself. The thump of uneven, heavy footfalls with the click of a cane told him who his visitor was. He'd already spoken to him last week. Well, argued more's the truth. It seemed the older he got, the more they had to debate over. He knew he wasn't being spiteful or willful, maybe just maturing.

The step and thump came close, then stopped.

The man sighed. "No warm greeting for yer father?"

Alex hmphed. "I gave ye yer warm greeting last week. What do ye come to trouble me over now, Da?"

His father pounded his cane on the packed earth once. "That was an awfully beautiful lass who just passed me on the way out. Too pretty to have tears running down her face."

Alex huffed. "She's earned them." There was a pause in their conversation.

His father shifted, and the cane whacked against the bars near Alex's back. "Don't tell me ye just sat there when she came to see ye. Did ye even speak to her?'

Alex turned and glared at his da. "Aye, said all that needed to be said."

His father tilted his head. "George spoke to ye?"

Alex stood. "Aye, about my case."

His da hit the cane to the floor again, causing dust clouds to puff up. "No, about Iris. George was to tell ye." Alex leaned his hands on the bars above him, dropping his head as a headache came on.

He mumbled. "No, I won't speak about her."

Roderick Alexander MacDougall yelled, "Ye little selfish bagbaw! Ye didn't see her did ye? Didn't bother turning around and look at her face?" He growled. "My own mistakes misinterpreting betrayal passed on to my son. What a web we weave." Alex raised his head. His father had only once taken this tone with him. When he'd failed the Fae, lost the Stone of Love, and caused Heather's death. He stared at his da, fearful of what error he'd made now.

His father's cane whacked the bars. "Lieutenant Tytler has been arrested, tried, and found guilty. The crown stripped him of rank and title. Given him his discharge and sent him back to his home in England with his measly tail between his legs like the dog he is."

Alex chuckled. "Good and well deserved."

His father raised the cane and rapped his fingers, hitting them, making him jerk back and yelp. "What was that for, Da?"

His da roared back. "For being an edjit!" He took a few deep breaths and limped closer to the cell as he hissed, "There's a reason Iris couldn't come see ye for weeks." He exhaled. "When they arrested Iris, they placed her with all the women they'd brought in. But Lieutenant Tytler sought her out. Separated her from the rest."

Alex moved back, his breath gone. Dizziness overcame him. No!

"Lieutenant Tytler's charges were assault and attempted rape. Had ye bothered looking ye'd see the bruising fading from her face."

Alex fell to his knees. "Attempted, ye said attempted."

His father rested on his cane. "Aye, after overseeing the case that released the women, Lord Erskine came personally to retrieve his daughter. He caught the Lieutenant just before…" Alex rocked back and sat hard, placing his head in his hands. He took deep breaths while *just before* echoed in his mind. Oh God, he'd sent her away—forever.

Lifting his gaze, he sputtered, "I must speak with her."

His da shook his head. "Ye can't. I had to bribe the guard for this one visit. Her father doesn't even know she's here." He chuckled. "Seems the lass has a lot of practice at sneaking out of her father's manor."

Alex tilted his head. "Ye brought her on yer own?"

His sire smiled as he leaned on his cane. "I've spent time with Iris. A lovely woman."

As his da sighed and dramatically rolled his eyes he stood taller. "Too bad ye messed this meeting up so badly. If only someone would speak to her on yer behalf." Alex stood reaching through the bars.

The older man stepped back fast, holding his cane up as he laughed. "Got yerself in a pickle now, don't ye, son?" He turned, swinging the cane, walking without a limp. At the door, he turned and smirked. Alex stood stunned. His da never needed the cane, yet he'd used one for as long as Alex could remember.

His father leaned on the cane again. "A fable has shown itself. A prince and false love found true in a maiden by a stream. A maiden's sacrifice. Only through love will ye find the way, laddie." The words from his da's letter to him about the Stone of Love fable showing itself. A signal that the Fae needed a MacDougall to find a Magic Iona Stone.

Alex's eyes went wide. "The fable, the prophecy."

His da nodded. "Have ye seen the Stone of Love? Balor?" Alex shook his head.

The older man eyed him. "Be wary, son. Yer time is upon ye."

Chapter 14

Alex stood flanked by a half dozen British soldiers with rifles ready should he decide to escape. He blew a laugh and stood at the entry of the courtroom he'd served as an advocate for the last two years. Yet this time, he entered as the accused.

This morning, when his father arrived with a fresh change of clothing and toiletries to make himself presentable after the over month-long wait for Lord Justice General Henry Graham from Edinburgh to come, he'd given a warning. "Son, that damned Tytler has returned to Glasgow and rallied his friends. His actions brought out all haters of anything Scottish. Convinced half the city, we are all out to oust the King again."

As he shifted his cane he spoke, "I met Lord Justice General Henry Graham yesterday. A fine man and a good friend to Lord Erskine. He's here for justice and doesn't like the dramatics Tytler has brought about."

His da lifted his cane and swung the stick through the air like a broad sword. "But no worries, Alex, we are prepared for Tytler and his overzealous friends."

When Alex entered the courtroom, forewarned didn't prepare him for the onslaught of insults and jeers shouted his way as he entered the courtroom.

"Damned filthy Scot!"

"Dirty pig should hang now!"

"You lost at Culloden. Die like the rest!"

The calls from the room drowned out Lord Justice General Graham's pounding his gavel as he sat on the dais. His mouth moved, but over the roar of the crowd, Alex couldn't hear him.

Alex held his head high and strode forward to the front. His gaze roamed over the people shoving to be near him, not one he recognized. After another few steps, his eyes lifted, and met Lieutenant Tytler's. No, Patrick Tytler's, as he stood behind the undulating crowd, the smirk clear on his face. Beside him, another set of men he recognized from the raid—all three out of uniform.

A hand touched his left arm, and when he turned, Mabina nodded and gave the Gaels sign, a finger in the forehead representing the Scottish unicorn as she faded back into the crowd. So, the Gaels were here to defend their leader. Alex took a cleansing breath as he moved to the boxed-in area with wooden railings for the accused. Of all the times he'd been in the courtroom, this box was the last place he thought he'd ever stand.

He glanced to his side, and George Hamilton nodded as he held his papers, ready for his presentation. His da, tall and proud as the Laird he was, sat next to Lord Erskine, who wore his regular clothing. Alex had seen Lord Erskine out of his court robes before, but never in this room.

A chill ran through him as Lord Justice General Henry Graham's voice cut through the crowd's deafening roar and the banging of the gavel. "Silence, I command silence." He pounded the gavel again, as Alex's heart beat with each strike. Would he truly be found guilty of high treason against the crown he'd sworn to serve?

As the crowd quieted, he breathed a short prayer.

"Please, God, of everything I've asked, let me serve Scotland again. I owe a debt to her."

The room quieted, and Lord Graham's scrutiny traveled the chamber. "Please note. I will not tolerate disruptions to the court. Those who cannot abide will be arrested."

Lord Graham settled his gaze on Alex. "Alexander Ewan MacDougall, you are charged with high treason against the crown. You have entered a plea of not guilty."

The crowd erupted again, and Lord Graham's gavel banged harder. "Silence!" He leveled his eyes on Alex. "You understand the charges against you?"

As the accused, Alex spoke clearly. "Aye, I do."

The courtroom broke into various yelling as Lord Graham's voice rose above all. "Another outburst, and I'll clear the room!" He stood and slammed his gavel. "I will have order!" He sat as the crowd quieted.

Lord Graham turned to the court solicitor. "Mr. Wright, your case, please?"

Alex's eyes traveled to his side, where the court advocate sat. George had mentioned that the solicitor, Anthony Wright, had campaigned hard for the case, and now he knew why. Patrick Tytler sat behind him, their heads bent in muttered consultation. So, Tytler had his hand in everything.

As the accused, Alex contemplated his position. The fight would be hard, and a win unlikely, but he had faith. He sat in his place beside George and mentally set himself up for the oncoming testimony, good and bad. He couldn't react, couldn't show emotion. The slightest sympathy shown for Scotland might work against him. He needed all the edges he could gain with this crowd.

Mr. Wright stood. "I call Patrick William Tytler."

Alex groaned inside. They started with the dramatics. But this might be good. If Lord Graham grew tired of the crowd's disruptions, he'd empty the court. Lord Erskine had done so many a time to keep order. He suspected Lord Graham had entered the courtroom with little patience for their theatrics. Wright's tactics were off for the judge he had. Alex smiled to himself. This may work out in the end. Tytler strode forward, confident in his step. He took the stand and faced Lord Graham with a smirk.

Mr. Wright stood in his place between the witness and the judge. "Mr. Tytler, please explain your previous position and duties to the crown for Glasgow."

The former officer adjusted his necktie. "As Lieutenant to the King's army, my duties involved enforcing the rule of the heathens of Scotland, the Jacobites." Murmurs flitted through the courtroom and then quieted. Tytler pulled on his cuffs. "I found out about the Gaels, the secret Jacobites, by following Alex MacDougall, and my suspicions about him proved correct."

Tytler pointed to Alex. "He is the leader of the remaining Jacobites in Glasgow and plans to overthrow the crown!" The man's face turned red as his voice rose. "He spewed his rhetoric for all and poisoned my betrothed, Iris Erskine." Alex's blood boiled, the nerve of the man. He'd been thrown out of the Hogmanay Ball at Lord Erskine's home before one and all for attacking Iris. All knew they'd never set a betrothal.

Lord Erskine stood, but George spoke before anyone could. "Objection, my lord. Hearsay! No one has spoken of Alex's treachery, and as Lord Erskine never confirmed the suit, and the lady never agreed. They'd made no formal engagement announcement."

Lord Graham nodded. "A truth I know of personally." He fixed his eyes on Tytler. "A warning, Mr. Tytler. Perjury will be met with swift justice. Try sticking with the facts. As a *previous* crown officer, I assume you know what that means?" The reminder of his office and insult of his removal delivered, Tytler could only nod. But his glare slid to Alex, and his eyes tilted into slits. So, the game was still on. What else did the man have planned since they'd shot down his first ploy so quickly?

Tytler stood tall as he spoke. "I followed Alex MacDougall, found him preaching against our King to his *Gaels,* and arrested them all." He swallowed. "It is as I have given in my report. His speeches spoke of Scotland's freedom, the right to wear the plaid, to speak their heathen language and out the English."

Mr. Wright waved his hand. "Thank you. Step down."

Tytler did, and when he passed Alex, he hissed, "You'll hang bastard." Alex only grinned. Lord Erskine played a large part in an order the parliament signed nearly two months ago preventing accused Jacobites from hanging without severe and multiple forms of proof. Unless the court advocate planned to lie during the entire case, the last thing that would happen to Alex was hang.

His father growled beside him. "Ye aren't a bastard." His da leaned over and spoke lowly, "None so blind as those who will not see." One of his ma's sayings, and true on more than one level. Alex was not only his da's son, but he was also his spitting image. Father and son for all to see.

The rest of the morning saw both of Tytler's lackeys testify the same as Tytler and a few officers Alex didn't recognize from the raid, likely bribed for more testimony against him.

Close to the midday break, Mr. Wright called his next witness. "I call Officer James Drake." Alex turned as Drake made his way from the back of the room. Dressed in his uniform, he moved into the box and stood tall. He swore in and faced Lord Graham. Had they gotten to him, too? Drake was of lower rank in the King's army and needed the coin. His position paid for his family. Alex's gut dropped. Tytler twisting his lackeys was one thing, but Drake's family needed him.

Mr. Wright droned out his question. "Officer Drake, your post with the King's Army is the bridge area. Please tell us all you know of the Gaels and their meetings."

James cleared his throat and started with a stutter, "I… I am a loyal officer to the King. I swore to do my duty and protect all the citizens." His voice strengthened as he spoke, "I swore an oath today to tell the truth. The truth is what you shall have from me." He took a deep breath. "The Scots who meet under the bridge are not Jacobites."

Gasps sounded around the room, but James continued speaking. "I've been under that bridge for four years. I watched them start with one or two, then grow into a group. They are all good people only interested in their way of life. No one speaks out against the King. They live in peace."

He sighed and slouched a little. "You see, it's the same way with tea. I like my tea hot with lemon. But my wife likes hers with cream. Same tea, but different." He glanced at Alex. "With the Scots, it's the same way.

Same life under the King's rule, but just a different flavor."

He faced Lord Graham. "I never stopped them as I never saw them as a threat. They are no more threat to you as I am." He nodded. "And that's all I have to say about it."

The Justice nodded back and turned to Mr. Wright, raising an eyebrow. "Any more witnesses?" Mr. Wright shuffled his papers, clearly flustered.

Lord Graham cleared his throat, and Mr. Wright jolted. "No, my lord."

Banging his gavel Lord Graham called out, "Till one thirty. Mr. Hamilton, we shall hear your case next."

All rose, and the court broke for midday on a positive note. The officer led Alex back to his cell, and the afternoon dawned with hope.

****

That afternoon Alex was led back into the courtroom to a much more subdued, smaller crowd. It seemed Tytler lost some of his supporters, but this was good.

Over the mumbles in the courtroom, Lord Graham spoke, "Lord Advocate Hamilton, your case?"

George called his first witness, Mabina McGee. She strode forward, swore in, and faced Lord Graham as George spoke. "Mrs. McGee, please explain your recollections of the gatherings held under the Clyde River bridge to the court." He and George had agreed not to call the meetings by their slang name, the Gaels, as the name insinuated the connection to the Jacobite cause.

Mabina smiled. "They wasn't planned, ye see. We all gathered as friends to talk about our lives, our culture, and how to keep it alive." She waved toward Alex. "Alex wasn't even in the first year of meetings anyway, so I don't know how ye accuse him of being the leader."

His friend folded her arms. "The truth of the start was a place for me to meet customers for pickups from the other side of the bridge, so they didn't have to come into town to my shop." She grumbled. "Not once had I heard anyone talk against the King. We all want peace and to live our lives."

The baker glanced at Alex. "I invited Alex MacDougall after word got around how he helped Scots in the courts." She faced Lord Graham. "A job he takes to heart he does."

George nodded. "Thank you, Mrs. McGee. Please step down, but remember you must stay in case the court has further questions."

As she moved down, she winked at Alex. The rest of the testimony progressed similarly. Other Gaels members came forward, testifying the same. Alex wasn't the start, no one spoke against the King, and everyone wanted to ensure that the Scottish culture survived. Plus, many looked forward to what the newsletters called a business boom for Glasgow, accrediting the new trade licenses granted for trade with the Americas. Others submitted written statements from the people he'd helped with his work for the courts. All praised his duty to the crown.

Near the end of the day, George stood and called his next witness. "I call Laird Roderick Alexander MacDougall." Alex knew George would call his father, but hearing his formal name caught his breath. His da called to testify for him. His heart swelled as he felt like a boy again, needing his da to save him. They'd discussed what would be said, but the fact still rocked him.

His sire lifted himself using his cane and limped to the box. His uneven gait was more pronounced. Now that Alex knew he didn't need assistance, he had to cover his mouth to hide the grin. Roderick was the best player, and Alex was glad he was on his side.

George stood and paced before the assembly. "Laird MacDougall, your son is Alexander MacDougall?"

His da chuckled. "Aye, I made him and caught him as he popped out of my sweet Mary." He stood tall. "Proudest day of my life. We had trouble getting one." He turned to the crowd and winked. "Had to keep at it. Practice makes perfect." The crowd laughed. Alex smirked. They were in for a performance now.

George blushed brightly and cleared his throat. "Your family serves the Campbells?"

His sire leaned on his cane. "Aye, a unique agreement it 'tis. I allow them to use Dunstaffnage Marina as a defense point. We have an agreement on my whisky trade, and I keep my ancestor's land." Roderick chuckled. "That is if the Campbell doesn't drink all of his supply of whisky profits." More laughter came from the crowd as Lord Graham huffed a laugh.

His da turned to the crowd. "The Heart of Scotland Whisky is the smoothest whisky ye'd ever let past yer lips." More chuckles met his statement.

George paced. "Thank you. We've noted your service to the crown."

As his da stood tall he squared his shoulders. "Aye, as is my son's to yer courts. The MacDougalls wish to see the people of Scotland survive. We all embark upon a new era, and the people are eager for this opportunity."

He thumped his cane. "Alex was the bridge we all

needed to help us navigate our way in dark times. It's time to forge ahead, together as a new Scotland, one with its culture while under the King's justice." Many "ayes'" and "yes's" replied to his statement. Lord Graham nodded and smiled.

George turned to face Lord Graham. "My case rests, my lord."

The lord banged his gavel. "Till two pm, tomorrow." George returned to his seat, and his father joined them.

Lord Erskine leaned over. "Good job, all. Tomorrow, closing statements, then the ruling."

As the guard led Alex away, his da nodded. "Good work, son. Keep yer hope and faith."

Chapter 15

Alex sat in the courtroom for day two of his trial. The court solicitor spoke rapidly with Tytler, seeming to argue. Lord Graham cleared his throat and eyed Wright, who glanced at Lord Judiciary's and then returned to the whispering Tytler. Wright waved him off, and as Tytler stood, his glare met Alex across the courtroom. The gleam in his eye sent a chill down Alex's spine.

Wright stood and addressed Lord Graham. "My lord, a new witness has come forward demanding to be heard."

George stood with a bark in his reply. "The court has no other witnesses listed."

Lord Graham waved both to sit. "Boys, I wish all to have a voice in this case. I'll allow it." Lord Graham waved to the court's solicitor. "Lord Wright, your witness?"

The man waved and the back doors opened, everyone shifted and gasped. Alex turned to a sight he was not prepared for. With her head held high and her hands clasped tightly before her, Lady Iris Erskine strode into the courtroom with Laurel following. As Iris stepped onto the stand, Laurel sat next to Alex's father.

Lord Erskine stood. "I object!" To his daughter, he hissed, "Iris, what are you doing here?" Iris stared straight forward and didn't acknowledge her father's outburst. Alex had his first good look at her face. Yellow splotches still marred her cheeks, and a slight hint of purple still trailed down her nose, but she looked regal, like a queen.

Lord Graham raised an eyebrow. "Lord Erskine, you have no authority in this court, and your daughter has willingly come forward. I understand she was present for much of the time when the accused was in question. I wish to hear her testimony."

Wright stood, and Lord Graham waved at him. "Sit, Lord Wright. I should like to question the lady."

Alex's eyes never left her since she entered the room. A blush rose on her neck, but other than that, she stood her ground. God, she looked stunning. Her dress hugged her curves, and her auburn hair caught the sunlight from the window. Her profile remained frozen, but her hands gave away her nerves as they shook slightly. A movement beyond her caught his attention. His eyes adjusted, focusing as Tytler shifted till he sat in the front row closest to Iris, a sneer pasted on his face.

Lord Graham's voice brought Alex's focus back to Iris. "Lady Erskine, you have given a statement. Sworn on its truthfulness. Is there something else you wish to add that I need to consider in making my judgment?"

Her lips trembled as she took a breath. "Yes, my lord. The court took a statement, but I didn't include everything I wished to say."

Lord Graham waved her on. "Please speak freely, My Lady."

She twisted her hands. "At first, the thought of attending the Scots meetings was to meet these dynamic people who seemed to love life." She brushed a stray hair from her face. "They love this land, its heritage, and all that Scotland is as a country." She breathed. "They refer to this land as a person, often calling her female as if she lives."

Her gaze met Lord Graham. "Never once did I hear anyone speak out against the crown, but only how these people who love such a harsh and beautiful land could ensure their culture survived."

She rested her hands on the railing framing her in the stand. "When I met Alex MacDougall, well, my reason for joining the meetings changed. Through his eyes and heart, I gained an insight few who aren't from Scotland see."

A tear escaped, but her voice spoke firmly. "Through Alex's work, he has ensured the people of Scotland got fair and honest treatment. Through his example, the people of Scotland have found a way forward, living within the King's rule while still being able to maintain the heart of Scotland. He showed them how to keep their culture while living lawfully."

Her voice wobbled as she spoke the next. "I not only fell in love with Scotland, I fell in love with Alex." She took a deep breath. "To take his life is to take Scotland's heart." She whispered the last. "And my own."

He heard all she said, all that her heart held dear, and fell in love with her all over again. Her voice pleaded for his life, telling him all about his love for Scotland and all he would do to see Scots living peacefully. But her heart pleaded for his love.

When she turned to him and her eyes met his, he couldn't turn away. "I may not be a maiden by a stream or a beauty with a magic stone necklace, but I am truly in love with you, Alex. Please forgive me." Her words stopped him. They were from the Stone of Love fable he'd told her.

She turned to Lord Graham as Alex jolted. Would Balor exact his revenge here and now? Maybe possess a human to do his bidding. His eyes shifted to Tytler, who sat glaring at Iris. Would Balor use Iris?

His father breathed in his ear. "The Fae wouldn't do anything in such a public place. Too many to witness, leaving too much to explain." He pulled his cane into his lap and gripped the shaft firmly. "Yet, keep an eye out. Evil is afoot."

Iris's voice spoke softly. "I wanted everyone to know Alex wasn't out to go against the King but to find a way to hold Scotland true while still living within English rule, lawfully." The room paused after her declaration. Almost as if they waited for something magical to happen.

Tytler stood and slowly clapped. "Well, well. His whore has spoken. And such sweet words recited from the Lord High Counselor's daughter in a pathetic attempt to save her lover." Murmurs spread through the courtroom. Some voices rose as heated words flew.

Lord Graham banged his gavel. "Mr. Tytler, you speak out of turn."

Tytler yelled as he moved, "I will have my vengeance, you bitch!" The flash of a knife caught Alex's eye. For Alex everything moved in slow motion.

Tytler drew a knife as he lunged into the box where Iris stood. She shifted but had nowhere to go, the railings trapping her in the small space. The courtroom filled with yells and screams, all mingling into one loud roar.

Alex stood and leapt toward Iris. His father moved before him as he drew a long, thin blade from his cane. Before Alex reached Iris, Tytler stumbled against the railing and cut her stomach. His father's sword connected with Tytler's knife. With the flick of his da's wrist, Tytler's bloody blade flew and skidded across the room.

Iris screamed and collapsed as Alex cleared the stand and caught her in his arms. "Ivy!" Guards swarmed the stand. Some pulled Tytler away and held him as others dragged Alex away from Iris, keeping him away from his love.

A couple of guards helped Iris to stand while she gripped her belly as blood soaked her fingers. "God, no. Please don't hurt my baby!" Alex's breath froze. He pulled hard against the guards' hold. His eyes connected with Iris's as tears streamed down her face. He couldn't help, hold, or tell her how happy he was she carried his baby.

Lord Graham's gavel beat fast as his voice carried over the chaos. "Order, I will have order!" The people in the courtroom fell silent.

Alex's focus moved to his father, who stood next to Lord Erskine, leaning on his cane, now whole. His da glanced around the room, and Alex followed his line of sight. Is Balor here? Is his moment at hand, here, now? When Alex's gaze returned to his da's, he shook his head. No, the Fae were not here.

He turned at Lord Erskine's bark. "Lord Graham, I must take my daughter to safety and care for her wounds."

Lord Graham nodded. "Of course, James, please see to your daughter. I've heard enough." With the courtroom in order, the guards released Alex. Iris stood between two guards with her head bent. Alex had to say something.

When they helped her down into her father's arms,

Alex stepped forward as his da's hand gripped his arm. "Another time, son, the court still waits for a verdict."

When Iris came even with him, he whispered. "Iris." She choked a sob as her father led her from the courtroom, with Laurel following. When Alex turned to face Lord Graham, he glanced to his right, and two guards held a struggling Tytler. Tytler would get what he deserved.

Lord Graham shifted in his seat. "Well, I've had enough theatrics. Arrest Patrick Tytler for disrupting court and attempted murder."

Tytler bellowed as the guards dragged him away. "Scot pigs will burn in hell!" The people in the courtroom shifted, some replying with jeers against Tytler.

The room settled again, and Lord Graham's gaze moved over the people. "I have heard all the testimony and read the charges against Alex MacDougall. Scotland's time of unrest has come to an end. New laws pass daily, improving life for both English and Scottish people. This city, as well as Edinburgh, has boomed with a surge of industry I've not seen before. The future is upon us, and as people, we must progress into a time of peace."

He sighed. "Under new revelations from the arresting officer, I fear his personal feelings of hate overruled good sound judgment." He lifted his gavel and banged the wood three times. "Alex MacDougall is innocent and will return to his post immediately, serving Scotland in Glasgow's courts. Dismissed." Cheers erupted in the courtroom. His father patted his back, and the only place he looked at were the doors where Iris had left. Was she well? Was their baby well?

****

Alex and his father rode into the stable yard of his townhome. "Da, I wanted to see Ivy! Why the hell can't I go see her?" Alex dismounted Oberon and handed the reins to his stablemaster.

His father doing the same with his mount replied, "Alex, ye will allow Lord Erskine to care for the lass. I am certain he will send word when you can see your bride."

Alex strode through the kitchen, yelling back at his father. "Bride? I haven't asked her yet!"

As they entered the foyer, his father whacked his cane on the bench. "Ye will marry the mother of yer child, Alex!"

Alex huffed as he picked up the post from the side table where the stack awaited him. "Of course, I'll marry her, Da, I love her. But I'd like to see her, know she fares well."

As Alex flipped through the many letters, John came down the stairs. "I heard about yer dramatic case. Congrats on yer freedom."

Alex stopped at an interesting letter—one in old, thick velum with a dark red seal of a dragon with its wings raised in flight. The seal was unfamiliar, yet he felt he'd seen the design before. A chill flashed over his body as his fingers moved over the parchment. Heady musk floated off the page, and he had to put his hand out to stop the dizzy spin of his head.

His father's voice came from afar. "Alex, what is that?" Alex broke the seal and opened the letter, noting its fold was an older type—one his grandma had used in her letters. When he gazed upon the open letter, a blank page glared back at him.

His da huffed. "That's strange."

The sound of a quill scribbling against the parchment filled the room, and words inscribed themselves onto the page as if written at that moment. His father stepped close and glanced over his shoulder.

Hello, lovesick pup,

Thought I'd forgotten ye? Think again, boy.

Ivy, such a lovely name. It's also called lovestone due to its tendency to grow over bricks and stones. Ivy clings to any surface, making it a perfect representation of wedded love and fidelity.

The words faded, and Alex's heart dropped as his words returned to haunt him. The quill sound filled the room again.

She's a beautiful woman, Ivy, or is it, Iris?

Yer pet name doesn't matter; she's not yer Ivy anymore.

Her blood is so red, her heart so pure. Why, I might take my ease on her while I wait for your arrival.

The words faded again as his father growled. "Balor, the bastard!" Scratches of a quill came to him again, and words appeared onto the paper.

Come, boy. Come get yer Ivy. Will The Stone of Love glow brightly for this one? Come to yer fairy hill, and let's see if ye have what it takes to get yer love back. Or will I kill this one as well? Heather was such a luscious kill. As sweet as the plant, but Ivy is so lively. I shall enjoy taking her soul, and yer babe's with it.

The words faded as Alex ripped the paper into bits with a yell. "God damn it! No! Not again and not Ivy!" He strode into the parlor and went straight to the mantel.

Over his shoulder, he bellowed. "John, get my plaid! If I go to battle, I go as a Scot!" His father followed him into the room as John's stomps shook the steps. A thump came from above, followed by the tread of John running down the stairs.

Alex bent, opened the bolt hole, and removed the chest holding the Brooch of Lorne. When he opened the box and pulled the brooch out, the Stone of Faith and the Stone of Hope glittered in the rays of dusk from the window.

John knelt in the middle of the room, folding Alex's plaid. "It's Balor? He's back?" His da marched to him without a limp, set his cane down, and took the brooch from him.

Alex kicked his boots off, stripped off his trews, lay on the floor, and belted on his plaid. He quickly pulled on his shoes, trying not to imagine Ivy in Balor's hands.

As he stood, his da helped him pin the brooch to his shoulder as he spoke. "Aye, the bastard is back. Always picking the worst time, too." His eyes connected with Alex's. "Yer grandma hated his perfect timing."

With the brooch pinned, Alex moved to pass his father, who stopped him with his hands on his shoulders. "Balor's powers have grown with an Iona Stone. Ye'll have to be stronger, smarter than ye were before, son."

Alex stopped, gazing back at his father. "I know, Da."

Patting his cheek, his da's voice came firmly. "Use yer will to overpower evil. Yer love will give ye power and strength." He nodded and released him. "Yer true love, Iris, will help power the stones. Use it."

His da hugged him. "Ye've grown into a fine man." He stepped back and sighed. "I have hope and faith in ye, son, but most of all, I love ye."

Tears welled as he took his da in a tight hug. "I as

well, Da."

He released his sire and moved past John, who stopped him with a hand on Alex's arm. "Ye need help?"

Alex stood tall. "No. I started this, and I will end it."

Chapter 16

As dusk settled over the city, the large man in the black suit with a dark, angular beard yanked Iris beside him. She pulled hard against his firm grip, but with her courtroom injury, plus his attack that overturned her father's carriage, and her waning strength, she couldn't gain control. The pain from her cut, combined with weakness, overshadowed her concern for her father and Laurel's wellbeing. Dizziness overcame her, and she fell, hitting her knees on the hard, cold ground.

The strange man bent and grabbed her face, reminding her of Lieutenant Tytler's grip. "Come, Ivy, the fun is about to begin."

Pulling her up by her armpits, the madman stood her as she wavered. "Yer lover is about to show. Ye'll want to witness what I have planned."

He positioned them beside a tree. As they turned and faced Glasgow, Iris recognized the location where the madman took her. This was the picnic spot Alex had brought her to those many weeks ago—the day after the Hogmanay Ball. The time he shared his hopes and dreams, his heart with her. Tears stung her eyes as she swallowed the lump in her throat.

The man brushed her hair from her face. "Don't cry, sweet Ivy. Alex will be here soon, and I'll get what I want. With the lack of response the MacDougalls have made to retrieve the Stone of Love, I'm itching for a battle."

He bent and kissed her lips. "Ye, my dear, make the perfect bait." He took the necklace he wore, a thick silver chain with a heart the size of a man's fist at the end, and placed the locket over her head. The pendant weighed down the necklace, making the item feel like a prisoner's chain.

Shifting behind her, the mad man held her hands in his tight grasp. "Now, play the part, my sweet. Yer true love approaches." The heart pendant warmed against her body as a red light glowed from inside.

Iris took a deep breath as love washed over her, highlighting her feelings for Alex. Thoughts flooded her mind: care, concern, and heated anger for harming someone he loved. *He loved* echoed in her mind, and that's when it dawned on her. These were Alex's emotions coming to her.

When she glanced back at the man holding her captive, his grin grew wide. "Now ye understand the power ye face, Ivy."

****

Oberon galloped up the hillside as the last rays of sun faded into the purple haze of impending darkness. The red glow Alex spotted halfway up the hill was now before him, lighting Ivy and Balor in a haunting red. *Ivy, my true love. Ye've made the Stone of Love glow.*

Alex bent his head and relished her emotions as they washed over him. Love, concern, worry, and fear all hit him hard. He took them in and stored them for the battle to come. He needed any edge he could get. He dismounted Oberon, drew his broadsword, and stormed toward Balor as the madman held his love captive.

Balor's hand came around Ivy's throat, holding a

knife there. "That's close enough, Alex. Don't want anything to happen to yer beauty while we—chat."

Alex yelled as he took a step. "There is nothing to say that my sword can't say for me, Balor!" Balor shifted the knife, nicking Ivy's throat and drawing a cry from her lips.

He jostled her in his arms. "I warned ye, boy."

The blood that trickled down his love's throat had him stopping as his eyes went wide. Her fear hit him hard. He needed to focus. Balor held control. Alex needed to shift the power to him and soon.

Balor chuckled. "She's nothing more to me than bait. The way to ye is only through her. Her life hangs in the balance like yer last love." Alex shifted his blade into both hands, squeezing the handle tight, desperately wanting to rush Balor and cut him, but Ivy's safety was more important than his blood lust. He stood waiting to learn Balor's game, then he would adjust his strategy. Slow and smart.

The evil man bent his head beside Ivy's. "Ye know, Ivy's blood smells so much more satisfying than yer last love. Heather, was it? While her death was nice, Ivy being pregnant makes hers much sweeter. Heather and Ivy, seems ye like plants."

His hand came around her stomach as he gripped her to him roughly, making Ivy cry out, "Alex, please help me!"

The Fae's hand moved roughly over her belly. "Ah, a female she will have. Still so small and young in the womb."

Ivy choked on a sob. "Please make him stop." Alex's anger built, but his care and love for Ivy flowed freely, and the stones on his left shoulder glowed—the green and blue blend into a beacon of aqua, reminiscent of a fresh ocean. With her hands free, Ivy struggled against Balor. In the scuffle, the knife nicked her shoulder, and she grabbed the cut as she screamed.

Balor dropped the knife, held his hand out, and a clear globe of light encircled Iris, freezing her in place. In the scuffle, her hair had come undone. Her dress still carried the stain of blood from her courtroom injury. Her eyes flashed in anger as her beauty radiated from her.

Alex took a step forward as Balor turned to him. "Why is it ye MacDougall men pick the feistiest women?" He sighed. "Now, I'll have to use part of my power to hold her." Alex had to fight his desire to run to Ivy, take her into his arms and away from this madness, away from Balor. Even in her frozen state she shifted her gaze to him—and he sensed Balor's hold weakening.

Balor's gaze moved to Alex's shoulder. "Ah, the Brooch of Lorne. It's been a long time since I've seen it. The Stone of Faith and the Stone of Hope look so lovely in its setting."

Alex doubted Balor could hold Ivy and fight against the stones' power—a plan formed. Patience was what would win today.

As Balor folded his arms, the globe holding Ivy still held. "Tell me, boy, do ye even know what ye have there? The power ye possess?" He chuckled. "Or is that just another pin to ye?"

As he shoved forward, Alex yelled, "Enough, Balor! The Stone of Love, it's time the gem returns to its rightful owner."

The king of the evil Fae grinned. "Yes, the time has come." He tilted his head. "Ye spent so much time on this hill pondering the future of Scotland. Would ye like me to show ye yer precious country's future?"

Alex pushed closer, anger and frustration surging within him at Balor's stall tactics. "Ye can't, and anything ye show me won't matter. I've come for the stone." He held his emotions in—he needed their power to strike true.

The Fae chuckled. "Ye lie. Yer feelings betray ye. Hate and anger build inside ye, but can ye control them to wield the stones' powers? Can ye use them to fight for yer love? Yer precious little plant?" Alex roared as he ran forward. Balor thrust his hand out as an energy force lifted Alex from the ground, causing him to fly backward, landing on his side with a grunt. Pain shot over his side, and he quickly scrambled to stand and face Balor again.

Balor's laugh filled the air. "I guess not." He chuckled, "Ye make this too easy, boy."

As emotions raged inside him, Alex thrust his left hand out. The stones in the brooch flashed as his arm glowed, and a bolt shot from his hand, hitting Balor, who folded over at the contact. The sphere holding Ivy flickered.

She moved against the edge and cried out. "Alex!" His assumptions were correct. Balor couldn't fight and hold Ivy prisoner at the same time.

The Fae focused on Alex as he moved to his side. "Well, well, well. The man has finally come out to play. And here I thought ye'd never grow up."

Good, this was what Alex needed, Balor's attention away from Ivy. The wind picked up and swirled around the hillside.

As Balor stood with both hands out, he waved them over the land. "Let me show ye, MacDougall, what the future of yer precious country is."

The Fae's hands moved in circular patterns before him, and the ground glowed in a gray, purple haze. "Let me show ye the demise of all ye hold dear, the Scots, the Gaelic language, the Scottish culture."

Gravestones flashed and came into view. First, there were a few, then many covering every open piece of ground on the hill. As Alex turned to look around him, every spot had a grave, some tall, some short. Different shapes crowded around Alex, pressing in on him until he stood on a tombstone laying before a grave marker.

Balor's chuckle rose over the building wind. "The fall of Scotland lays at yer feet, boy. All from yer failed attempt to find true love in Heather." The wind stopped as leaves fluttered to the ground that still held a ghostly glow, casting the graves in a haunting light.

Ivy whispered, "Dear God."

Balor's voice spoke softly, "Here is yer future, boy. They call this Scotland's city of the dead."

Around him, every part of the hillside held a grave. From his perch on top to the cathedral below. Even to his left, down the backside of the slope held headstones. Thousands covered the ground, thousands of dead Scots.

As Alex held his sword before him, he faced Balor and roared. "This is not true. It's nothing more than a spell to affect my emotions. Raise my fears and use them against me in battle."

Alex stepped off the stone and stormed around the headstones as he progressed toward his nemesis. "It won't work, Balor. I come for ye!" He ran the rest of the way with his sword, held ready to strike Balor down. The ground shook as Balor's grin grew, and the sound of breaking rocks reached Alex. Something grabbed his ankle, and he stumbled. When he looked back, a form broke through the grave and rose before him. More fractures sounded in the night as bodies rose from the graves, each wearing rags that hung on their bodies. All coming for Alex.

Balor's bellow came over the melee. "The future calls them zombies. I like to refer to them as *my* army of the dead." Alex swung at one, and the form crumpled to the ground; another grabbed his back. He shook that one off and turned with his sword, cutting the body in half. A woman's screeching form came at him, and he ran her through. One after another and another came at him— some taking hold of him as he cut them down in the action.

Ivy's voice carried over the rumble of attackers. "Alex, more come. It's too many!"

As Alex swung his sword side to side, striking each figure that charged at him, he shouted, "The locket, Ivy!'"

He swung again, taking down another screeching woman. "Inside is the Stone of Love." Ivy's hands picked up the heavy pendant. The light grew brighter as she held it, casting her in bright red. Alex cut down another body as one jumped on his back.

As he turned and thrust his back against a tall headstone, crushing the zombie on his back, he shouted with each shove. "The—*wham!*—fable—*wham!*—the— *wham!*—glowing stone—*wham!*—yer emotions— *wham!*—power it—*wham! Bam!*—magic stone."

With his last shove, the form on his back finally gave way, and another punched his face. His fast reflexes had him punching back, and the head flew off the body as the part crumpled to the ground. Alex felt Balor's powers shift—the Fae's energy rose as he commanded more bodies from the graves to attack.

He glared at Balor who chuckled, and his arms moved in a circular motion again. "That's it, boy, fight me like a man."

When Alex turned to check on Ivy, she'd removed the stone from the locket and held the gem in her hands. He curled his left hand into his heart as his right hand wielded his blade, keeping the zombies at bay. He poured all his love into his heart. His mind cleared as his sword continued to swing.

As Alex reached out to Ivy's mind, to her heart he pleaded, *Ivy, please trust me. Pour all yer emotions, good and bad, into the stone. On my war cry, throw yer emotions all at Balor.* She nodded.

A bark came from Balor. "It won't work. She doesn't know how to use the power of the stones."

Balor's voice strained in his efforts to fight with energy. "Ye brought me the Brooch of Lorne filled with the Stone of Faith and the Stone of Hope! When I take them from ye, The Stones of Iona will complete my destiny, giving me the power to rule the realms."

The evil Fae grunted with the effort to speak and control so many of his dead army. "Yer failure to Scotland will be complete!"

With a swing and a turn using his blade to take out more zombies, Alex focused on his emotions, the love, hate, frustration at the English, and his fears. Ivy rang in his mind as her emotions poured over him. Her hope flared as his emotions flowed into her, giving her power and strengthening her faith in him and them.

His stones glowed white, and he flung his left hand out, yelling the MacDougall battle cry. "*Buaidh No Bas.*

Victory or Death."

As he glanced up, Ivy held her chin tucked to her chest as she held the Stone of Love. Her right hand flung out palm up, casting a red stream of energy from her, hitting Balor's left side as Alex's energy hit Balor's right. Balor's head dropped back as his arms flung wide.

As the zombie army froze, Alex channeled his emotions, building power and pouring the energy into his arm before striking Balor, who rose from the ground, floating ominously in the air. The evil Fae turned, rotating his arm in Ivy's direction. A white bolt shot at her, striking her in the sphere. She cried out and fell to her knees. Her red energy stream vanished, but the Stone of Love still glowed. Alex refocused his energy. As he dropped his sword, he brought both hands forward, combining his energy into both.

He stormed toward Balor, who stared down at him. "Ye will not win."

Alex gathered all his love for Ivy and Scotland and flung his emotions out at Balor. "I already have. Go to hell!" A bright bolt flew from him, hammering Balor, who exploded in a flash of white light making him disappear.

As Alex fell to his knees, all the energy he had left in him drained. Weakened, he lifted his head as the army disappeared. Slowly, the graves, headstones, and markers faded as the gray, purple light dimmed and then vanished.

After a time, the wind blew softly over the hill that had returned to normal. The only light left was the Stone of Love, and when Alex turned to gaze at Ivy, the red light flickered and faded as her body crumpled to the ground.

Alex whispered, "Ivy?" He rose on unsteady legs and stumbled to her. He tripped and fell, then rose again, crawling the last of the way to his love. She lay on her side, one hand curled into her chest, holding the Stone of Love, which glowed no more. Her other hand stretched out in her last attempt to help him banish Balor.

As he grabbed that hand, the chill of her skin had him grasping her, rolling her over. "Ivy? No, no! Not again!" He took her in his arms and shook her as her hand on her chest fell away and released the Stone of Love. He bent, gathering her to him as tears gathered and spilled down his cheeks.

He yelled, "Not again. Balor didn't kill my love again!"

Alex sat and held her to his heart, rocking as pain washed over him. His Ivy lay limp in his arms, taken in the war of the stones.

Shifting her until her head rested on his shoulder, he stroked her face. "I'm sorry, Ivy, I love ye." She took a breath and stirred in his arms.

Alex choked with a sob. "Ivy?"

His love's eyelids fluttered and opened with a deep breath. "Alex? Is the fight over?"

Her fingers brushed away his tears as he spoke. "Aye, love. 'Tis over." He picked up the Stone of Love and held the heart before them.

Iris took the dark gem from him. "The Stone of Love glows no more."

Alex kissed her. "It did before ye used all its power. Ye are my true love."

Her eyes connected with his. "Yer maiden by the stream." She glanced at the red heart stone. "I had the strangest vision. A small, beautiful blonde woman, dressed in all white, flew before me with translucent wings shaped like a butterfly. She told me my time wasn't upon me. Said I had a destiny to fulfill." Her eyes went to his shoulder. "She showed me your pin. Told me what I had to do with the Stone of Love once I woke."

Ivy reached for the Brooch of Lorne, her fingers rounding the side until the secret compartment opened. She placed the Stone of Love inside and closed the brooch.

Alex shifted her till they lay back against the tree like they'd done on their picnic day. "Well, if yer account is correct and based upon my grandma's description, I think ye just met the MacDougall Fae, Brigid." Ivy shivered in the chill of the night, and Alex sat forward as he took the ends of his plaid and wrapped them in a warm cocoon. She hummed as she curled into him. They sat together for a moment.

Ivy tilted her head till their eyes met. "The fable you told me, the Stone of Love. Is it true?"

Alex brushed the hair from her face. "Aye."

Her gaze moved to the brooch on his shoulder. "The other stones, they are magic as well?"

He bent and kissed her forehead. "Aye, it's part of the MacDougall duty to the Magic Iona Stones. We protect them for the Fae."

She huffed. "That man, Balor, he was a Fae?" Alex nodded as she spoke again. "The bodies, the dead people?"

He rested his forehead on hers. "Not to worry, my love—they are gone." Ivy sat briefly, and her mouth opened again, but Alex kissed her. Softly at first, then deeper, tasting her, relishing her warmth as her heart beat with his.

She hummed, then sat up. "The power we used together made the energy stronger. It's how we won, right?"

As dawn warmed the sky, Alex squeezed her once. "Aye, and it's our way forward together. The joining of Scotland and England in marriage."

Ivy tilted her head. "Alex, are you asking me to marry you?"

He grinned as he kissed her, whispering into the kiss. "Marry me, Ivy."

She pulled back. "Ivy, not Iris?"

Alex brushed his fingers on her cheek. "To me, ye shall always be my lovestone, my Ivy." His hand moved to her belly. "And our girl, my Holly."

Ivy smiled. "Holly and Ivy, I like it."

As the sun rose and orange and red hues lit the sky, Alex held her tightly. "Our love will show the way to a new Scotland."

Ivy rested her head on his shoulder as a new day dawned. "Aye, that sounds nice."

Chapter 17

After two and a half months of a frenzy of planning on her mother's part, Iris woke to a bright June morning—her wedding day. She lay there a moment, reflecting on the last few weeks. After the confrontation with Balor, the evil Fae, Alex took her to his townhome to see to her wounds. Later that morning, when she arrived at her family's home, much to her relief, her father and Laurel had suffered only minor injuries in the attack on the carriage. Said carriage didn't survive the attack, but her father relished the opportunity to purchase a newer design as her mother beamed at the chance to parade around town in the latest style. After the shock of her unexpected pregnancy wore off, the promise of marriage and a grandbaby set her parents into motion, which quickly brought her to this day—her wedding day.

Laurel bounced into her room as Iris's maid, Lily, set her breakfast tray beside her.

Now, her companion and not maid, Laurel twirled and landed on the bed. "Yer wedding day! It's finally here!" She sat up. "I can't wait. Yer mother swears this will be the summer event in Glasgow society!" She sighed. "And I am to be yer maid of honor."

Iris grinned at her friend. "Yes, well, the fact that your wedding in our garden will be next week has nothing to do with your excitement."

Laurel stood and swiped a sweet bread from her

tray, nibbling on it. "Well, aye!"

Iris picked up her teacup and sipped it, peering at her friend over the rim. "Or the fact only yesterday you figured out you carried yours and John's baby."

Laurel sat on the bed as she finished her respite, licking her fingers. "Should I tell him before or after the wedding?"

She stood and pointed a finger at her dearest friend. "After, please." Lily held out her day gown and helped Iris out of her dress and into it. The skirt easily covered the slight bump of her pregnancy.

Iris sat again and waved her hand at Laurel. "I wouldn't rob my mother of her carefully planned event of the year. Not that the Hogmanay Ball wasn't an event people spoke of for months, but she plans to outdo that one with my wedding."

Laurel nodded. "Aye, ye are right. Yer mom on a mission can be quite formidable." She chuckled. "But she planned my wedding as well. A gift to me from yer da for caring for ye so well."

Iris smiled. "Well, living in Alex's townhome and raising the kids together will be nice." She glanced at Laurel. "Do you think you'll have a boy or a girl?"

Laurel grinned as she rubbed her belly. "A girl, for sure. I feel it in my bones."

For Iris, the rest of the day passed in a blur of preparations. A bath, hours drying her long hair in the sun. Later, she had afternoon tea with her mom, who cried tears of joy at the idea of her nuptials and the promise of her granddaughter to pamper. Soon, she'd dressed and stood before the gleaming new carriage with her father's hand helping her inside. He climbed in after she'd adjusted the mountains of fabric that made up her wedding dress and train.

Lord Erskine rapped the ceiling, and the carriage shifted then moved on toward Glasgow cathedral for her highly anticipated wedding with what the news sheets claimed was "Scotland's most desired bachelor and treasure, Alexander MacDougall, nabbed by an English flower, Iris, *Ivy* Erskine."

She giggled, and her father tapped her arm from across the seat. "Iris, I am happy to see you smile this day."

Iris reached for his hand. "I as well, father."

Her father grinned. "You do truly love him?"

As her face heated, she replied, "Yes, father. More than I can say."

He squeezed her hand. "I am glad to hear it. All we've ever wanted for you was your happiness, and I doubt there is a better man for you in the world."

Iris beamed at her father. "Thank you."

She glanced out the carriage window as the sights of Glasgow flew past. Almost every shop had closed for the event. While the wedding in the church held guests, her father had insisted on a picnic for the entire city. He, Lord Advocate of Scotland for Glasgow, insisted they share in the celebrations. The shared picnic was to take place at one of all the places, the hillside park behind the cathedral.

In the weeks leading to the wedding, Iris had taken most days to lunch with Alex. Only three days before, they'd picnicked on their *fairy hill*. As they approached the hillside, riding Oberon with the saddlebags stuffed for a picnic, two men dug a hole in the ground.

Alex stopped his horse as he called out. "Ye there, what do ye build on the hill?"

Both men turned as one called back. "Build?" He waved to the graveyard beside the chapel across the stream. "The graveyards are all filled Mi'Laird. The city said to bury the dead in the park." He wiped his forehead with a rag. " 'Tis to be the new graveyard." Iris glanced up at Alex with a catch in her breath, and Alex's jaw clenched. He nodded to the men and rode on to their tree. He swung his leg over the front of the saddle, landing sure-footed.

He turned and eased her down from Oberon. "Alex, do you think that's what Balor showed us? A large graveyard and not the complete desolation of Scotland?"

As Alex held her in his arms he spoke, "One can only hope so, Ivy." He sighed and glanced at the men, then the city beyond. "I certainly hope to make our version so."

At her hum, he glanced back at her as she spoke, "You will make your dream so, Alex. I know you will." The memory faded as the carriage stopped before the cathedral doorway.

Her father exited and held his hand to her. "Come, daughter. I am certain your groom awaits." Beyond him, the crowd gathered on the hill, tables filled with tasty offerings from everyone in attendance. Iris gathered her skirts and exited the carriage.

Laurel came to her and hugged her. "I couldn't wait. John knows and is so happy!" She stepped back and helped Iris spread her skirt and train out.

Iris smirked, knowing Laurel wouldn't wait. "Well, your news will give us all something extra to toast tonight." Laurel smiled and took her place before Iris for the entry as her father moved beside her. He coughed and sniffed. Was her steadfast father emotional?

She glanced at him, and he wobbled a grin. "I am very proud of you, daughter. Alex is a great man, and I know he will make you happy."

Tears built, and she slipped the handkerchief she'd secreted in her sleeve to dot her eyes as she spoke, "Aw, Father. I love you."

He bent and kissed her cheek. "I love you, daughter."

The door opened, and the organist's music rose, combined with bagpipes, as Laurel began her entry. When they walked forward, Iris had her first view of Alex at the pulpit waiting for her.

When their gazes connected, he smiled as his eyes roamed her gown, his first view of her in her mother's design. When his regard returned to hers, his grin was broad. His outfit, the same he'd worn for the Hogmanay Ball, made her legs go weak at the sight of his bare knees as they always did. He'd asked her if he could wear his clan's tartan for the ceremony, and she'd told him she'd be sorely disappointed if he didn't. John stood beside him, similarly, garbed in his blue plaid, his eyes only for Laurel, who strode before them as the maid of honor.

Alex had insisted they decorate the cathedral with holly and ivy for the occasion. Once her mother heard the reason, the source of Iris's nickname, Alex won the woman's devotion as she sobbed, claiming the moniker was the most romantic thing she'd ever heard.

As her father walked her down the aisle, she recognized many of the people she'd come to know so well in her time in Glasgow. People from the Gaels meetings sat intermingled with many she'd met from the English society in town. A blending that she and Alex had hoped for. As she neared the end of the aisle, Alex's parents sat in the front row on her right, Laird Roderick and Lady Mary MacDougall, beaming as their oldest son married. To her left, her mother dabbed her eyes with a handkerchief. The Tafts sat behind her as Mrs. Taft dabbed a kerchief to her eye. As she stepped toward Alex, she sensed she strode to her future—a future with the love of her life.

When her father passed her off, he addressed Alex, "Treat my daughter well."

Alex nodded. "I will hold her to my heart always." He took her hands in his and kissed them. Her gaze held his as the time came for their vows. They'd written their own, not just for them but an example for all the people attending.

The pastor turned to her smiling, and she took a deep breath to recite her vows. "From this day forward, let us laugh together, plan together, let us find our favorite places, and go together. Let us enjoy the sunshine and the rain, being alone and in crowds together."

Alex nodded when she finished and squeezed her hands as he spoke his. "Let us share our minds, thoughts, goals, values, and dreams. Let us develop these within ourselves without restriction or loss of freedom. Thus, our two souls may wander together as they develop in freedom." They'd agreed the end would be in unison, as the people should as well.

She eyed him as they took a breath speaking as one. "As we share our lives, as we walk through life together, know my love is yours. From this day forward, together, let us love!"

Alex turned them to the crowd and announced before the minister had a chance. "All of Scotland, my wife, my heart, my true love, Ivy MacDougall!" He kissed her hard as the cathedral broke into cheers. Alex led her out into the afternoon's warm rays as Laurel and John followed.

On the church steps, John patted Alex on the back. "Can ye believe it, both women expecting? We'll have a house full of kids before ye know it!"

Alex turned and touched John's shoulder. "It's how I dreamed this would be, friend."

Not waiting, Alex took her to the top of the hillside. Along the way, many congratulated them—some from the Gaels and others from Alex's work in the courts. When he came to the tables, he grabbed a drink, handed her one, and turned as the wedding guests filtered up the hill.

Lifting his glass, he called out to the crowd. "To my love and the future of Scotland!" A cheer rose as everyone gathered around. Alex shifted them back and moved toward their tree off to the side. He took her before him and turned them till they gazed out at Glasgow—the view from the cathedral to the river Clyde, the city's breadth.

He whispered in her ear, "To ye, Ivy. My love."

She turned into his arms. "To us, our family."

****

A baby's cry woke Alex to a chilly Christmas morning at Dunstaffnage Castle. He rose and picked up four-month-old Holly from her crib as she let loose another screeching wail.

Ivy sleepily rolled over. "Your daughter has your lungs, husband." She settled against the pillows as Alex handed their daughter to his wife, who situated her for feeding. He lay next to his wife and child, who desperately latched on and ate with gusto.

Ivy laughed. "And your appetite."

His finger trailed his daughter's cheek as he marveled at his family. The day she'd arrived rose often in his mind.

He'd been in the middle of a court hearing, and his stable master, Will, burst through the doors. "Alex, it's Ivy."

His heart dropped now as his stomach had that day. It turned out Ivy had been shopping with his parents, who visited her near her due date to be present for the birth, when her pains came. Ivy had nearly scared Will to death. Alex had rushed to her side, fearing the worst, and barely arrived in time to hold his wife as Holly popped out impatient to greet the world. His father toasted the arrival, claiming Alex had done the same. When his mother heard Holly's first cry, she'd covered her ears and claimed she had to be Alex's child with that set of lungs. That moment was the happiest day of his life, after his wedding day. As Ivy shifted Holly on her shoulder, the baby let out a loud belch.

Alex patted the child's back. "Aye, that's my girl."

He moved to stand, but Ivy's hand stopped him. "Today's the day. Alex, are you ready to say your final goodbyes?"

As Alex sat back, he took his wife and child into his arms. "I am ready to say goodbye to my past and greet my future. Ready to bless our child and celebrate the many gifts Christ has graced us with."

He kissed her lightly. "Come, wife, dress. We soon meet my parents, the MacArthurs, and Minister O'Donnell at the chapel."

All too soon, bundled against the early morning chill, the group made the short walk to the Chapel in the

Woods. Roderick and Mary led the way. His da's gait was uneven as he walked with the cane. Maybe he did need the support some days, as today he leaned on it. Alex and Ivy followed as his wife carried Holly, who was merely a roll of fur to keep the Christmas morning chill away. John and Laurel followed, her moving slowly with a rounded belly. John Sr., with his wife, Rose, trailed after. They'd decided Holly's christening would be the last event the Chapel in the Woods held before they let the building fall to ruin to hide the Stones of Iona from the evil Fae.

As they approached, Minister O'Donnell stood at the door. He nodded and didn't speak until all were in the nave. As Alex entered, he glanced around at the splendor of the Chapel his mother had decorated in her usual flair. Candlelight flickered as greenery filled with mistletoe adorned every surface. Her favorite at Christmas. Sunlight filtered through the circular windows and encircled the altar in a halo of light, making the scene seem like God blessed this moment just for them.

When they all stood before the table, his gaze moved to the recently packed dirt behind it. Yesterday he and his father buried the Brooch of Lorne on the hillside beside the chapel. They placed the Stones of Iona in the crypt beneath the holy building, their final resting place guarded by the MacDougall ancestors as each lay in their eternal rest.

Katheryn MacDougall, Ewan's younger sister and the First Lady of Dunstaffnage Castle before his marriage to Anne, held the Stone of Love in a necklace designed for her. This treasured piece was worn for generations by each Lady MacDougall—until now. The

Stone of Hope, Heather MacArthur, Alex's mistaken love held to honor her sacrifice given to the stones and serve as a beacon of hope for all. Before sealing the crypt, Alex had paused and said a short prayer for her soul, hoping she'd find peace. The Stone of Faith, Ewan MacDougall held, to represent his dedication to the MacDougalls in settling and building Dunstaffnage Castle.

Alex turned placing his arm around Ivy, who held their daughter, his gaze encircling his family in warmth and love. When his eyes met his da's, Alex nodded, and his da nodded back. Minister O'Donnell smiled in his warm, usual way.

The clergy dipped his hand in holy water and then placed his wet palm on Holly's head, murmuring, "I baptize thee Holly Anne MacDougall in the name of the Father, the Son, and the Holy Spirit." When the chilled water touched her forehead, Holly let out a wail that rocked the rafters.

Alex's da chuckled. "She's definitely yer daughter, Alex." All in the chapel laughed, breaking the somber moment and easing the tension in the room.

Minister O'Donnell patted Alex on the back and turned to his da. "Well, that's it, Roderick. Ye want them to take down the décor before we lock her up?"

As his da nodded, his ma, Mary, touched his arm. "No, I want the chapel to remain just as it is now, decorated my favorite way. If I must leave my holy building, this is how I want to remember my chapel."

His da bent and kissed her cheek. "As ye wish, my love." Minister O'Donnell shuffled about the space, blowing out the candles, and Alex felt his throat close. Today would be the last time they'd see the inside. His gaze connected with his ma's as she wiped a tear away. This was her special place, where she'd fallen in love with his da and shared many ups and downs. But as he watched his da pat her hand, he knew they'd be all right. They always were.

As the clergy held the family bible and led the group out of the building, Ivy tapped his arm. "You okay?" He blinked back tears as they moved to the door.

When they all cleared the doorway, O'Donnell closed the doors with a thud. The click of the latch echoed as he locked them.

Alex took a deep, cleansing breath. "Aye, I am." The group stood there for a moment in the cold Christmas morning. His ma's soft sobs carried in the air as his da took her into his arms, his cane forgotten in his hand. Everyone stood still. The wind blew, rustling the trees as a bird cooed from nearby.

His da was the first to break the silence. "All of ye, dry yer tears. There's nothing to worry about or be sad over. Ye should all be happy. Today is the start of our future. Without the chapel falling into disrepair, Colin MacDougall from the future doesn't meet Bree, and they don't come back in time to save ye, Alex."

He turned to Mary. "And ye, Mary, my love." He took a deep breath. "Without the chapel falling into ruin, they won't save us and all we hold dear."

His ma nodded as she dried her tears. "Aye, husband. One day, the chapel will rise again, and I know I will see my chapel from heaven. We have hope, faith, and love, and that's all we need."

Ivy spoke as she held Holly, "This is the cycle of life."

Alex kissed her forehead. "Aye, our future only awaits us."

A word about the author...

Margaret Izard is a multi-award-winning author of historical fantasy and paranormal romance novels. She spent her early years through college to adulthood dedicated to dance, theater, and performing. Over the years, she developed a love for great storytelling in different mediums. She does not waste a good story, be it movement, the spoken, or the written word. She discovered historical romance novels in middle school, which combined her passion for romance, drama, and fantasy. She writes exciting plot lines, steamy love scenes and always falls for a strong male with a soft heart. She lives in Houston, Texas, with her husband and adult triplets and loves to hear from readers.

You can email me at
info@margaretizardauthor.com
www.margaretizardauthor.com

Thank you for purchasing
this publication of The Wild Rose Press, Inc.

For questions or more information
contact us at
info@thewildrosepress.com.

The Wild Rose Press, Inc.
www.thewildrosepress.com